ASYLUM EXILE

Martyn Rhys Vaughan

Published by
Llyfrau Cambria Books, Wales, United Kingdom.
Cambria Books is a division of
Cambria Publishing.
Discover our other books at: www.cambriabooks.co.uk

To Penelope

who I searched for through all the probabilities.

Chapter One

Dexter Ward knew that he should be dead. He remembered the terrible noise, the sudden feeling of intense heat, the redness filling his entire field of vision, followed seemingly instantly by blackness. And then – normality. No angels; no demons; no Elysian fields or boiling sulphurous pits; just his table with his handgun lying on the surface among the whisky stains.

He picked it up. It was cold. He examined it more closely. No shot had been fired.

But that was impossible. He knew that a few seconds earlier that he had put the muzzle to this right temple and fired. He should be dead; dead as the proverbial. But he was not.

On the table next to the cold gun were some small cardboard boxes that contained partially used blister packs. He picked them up sequentially and stared dully at the names on the boxes: lurasidone; aripiprazole, haloperidol. How was it that these medications worked fine on all other people with his condition but had no effect on him whatsoever, except a general feeling of lassitude. Could any of them cause hallucinations? he suddenly wondered. Could they have made him think he had shot himself when he had not? He began reading the list of side effects of the nearest medication but gave it up after a few minutes. There seemed to be no end to the possible side effects, but vivid hallucinations were not among them. In any case he had *wanted* to end it all.

He leaned back in his chair and re-ran the events of his recent past

He had decided on suicide as the only way of getting the black dog of depression off his throat. He was an excellent software engineer, but he could not hold down a job. They all started the same way, with him impressing his bosses with his skill and appetite for work; with him rapidly becoming one of the team with his endless supply of jokes and unlikely,

1

but always amusing stories. In the after-work sessions in the wine bars there always seemed to be a leggy blonde slinking her way to the front of his admirers.

And then inevitably the problems would begin. The jokes would stop suddenly; the amusing stories would falter to an inconclusive end; the leggy blondes would drift away after a few encounters – some more memorable than others. Then would come the day when a boss would say the ineluctable words: 'Dexter – could I have a word with you in my office, please.'

And that would be that. Another period of unemployment. It was no good playing the illness card – his bosses wanted employees without any problems. They didn't mind employees having uncontrollable bi-polar disorder as long as they didn't bring it into the office.

His wife had said she could handle it. And so, she could – for five years. Gradually her smiles became thinner, more forced. She became less interested in dealing with his black days. Then came the day when she suddenly snapped: 'Not this shit again! For God's sake Dexter pull yourself together and act normal!' She had booked more and more sessions with her personal trainer until the day came when he came home from the pub and found a note pinned to the wall planner: 'Had to go Dexter. I need a man like Karl I can rely on. Hope you can handle your problems. Remember I did love you. Siobhan.'

It had been inevitable, he supposed, Siobhan had liked fun in her life, lots and lots of fun. He had supplied that when they had first met but, in those days, his black days were fewer and shorter and she had put it down to him being a moody guy.

What was the cliché? A downward spiral? Well, he had certainly been in that. And now he was in a one room flat in a managed complex, living on social security with his only friend being the whisky bottle. It was still single malt: he had hung on to that one shard from his earlier life, but it had stopped providing him with any real pleasure quite a while ago.

Obviously, a man like him shouldn't have been in possession of a handgun but there were ways and means. He had polished and cleaned it and taken it with him in the days when he had a car and fired it at unoffending trees when no-one was looking. Ammunition was a problem – but there were ways and means.

And he *had* picked it up. He *had* put it to his right temple. He *had* fired it.

But he had not. There was the evidence of the cold gun. And his continuing life.

He went to the bathroom and cocked his head so he could get an oblique view of his temple. Not a scratch. A morose face looked back at him. In its way it was a handsome face belonging to a reasonable looking man in his late thirties. A mop of curly black hair with no white hairs or signs of the dreaded M.P.B. Grey eyes; a fairly straight nose; a squarish jaw.

What more could the girls want? Perhaps a stable mind behind the face, he thought after a few more moments of self-inspection. Beaten by the paradox of continued Earthly Existence he returned to the living room. Perhaps God had sent one of his angels to intervene and stay the fatal shot. Who the hell knew?

Slumping on his shabby sofa he picked up yesterday's paper looking for confirmation that the world was still sane. He scanned the front page – no, there was no mention of invading Martians or strange diseases that had resurrected the dead or turned all the goldfish in the world purple. He turned page after page. The usual stuff about the Royal Family or chaos in Westminster; just as he had remembered it. He reached the final page and re-read the highlights of yesterday's soccer match.

And then it was that he frowned. The match had been a four-two win for Arsenal, he remembered that clearly, being an Arsenal fan. So why did the paper say it was a four-four draw? There was no way Liverpool could have come back from that deficit so late in the match that the papers had printed the wrong result.

And even if they had, this was the same paper that he had been reading last night. And it had unquestionably, definitely said four two to Arsenal.

He flung the paper across the room. This was madness, literal madness. He was going mad. His illness had taken a new and sinister turn and he was entering a world of his own making. His previous condition had been nothing to this! What could he do to halt the slide into drooling insanity?

He walked back and forth in the room for quite some time; not knowing what to do; not knowing what to think. In the end he ordered a takeaway and sat limply on the sofa. When his meal finally arrived, he

3

thought for a second before opening the carton. Would a strange unearthly fruit be revealed or a multi-legged insectoid something-or-other? But no, it was the Chinese stir-fry that he had ordered.

Ward sat silently after the meal and the obligatory can of lager. He reviewed the strange day once more and decided that entire series of events must be due to the stress he was under. He was unemployed – yet again – and his glamorous wife had left him. Anybody would show signs of trouble under that pressure! And despite what the labyrinthine notes for his medications had said it was not impossible that under certain circumstances they could generate confusion and mild hallucinations. He had indeed decided to end it all but quite clearly, he had not gone through with it. His mind had conjured up the feeling of what it would be like to place a handgun to one's temple but the drive for self-preservation must have kicked in and he must – *must*! – have put the gun back down on the table.

That was it. There could be no other explanation.

He had a medical condition certainly but so did millions of people throughout the world. He was not alone. No doubt somebody in Beijing or Ottawa was going through the exact same thing right now. They were his comrades in adversity although he would never meet them. He raised the empty lager can in a mock salute.

'Here's to us guys. It's you and me against the world.'

He felt a lot better after that. He put the gun away in its drawer. He knew he should have a locked cabinet but as far as he was aware the authorities did not know about his unauthorised weapon. He decided to turn in even though it was not particularly late – his shredded nerves needed sleep's healing balm.

But as he slept strange visions paraded through his mind. A small woman with hair that was sometimes raven-black; sometimes auburn. And strange tall, thin, ungainly men with hooded faces. He did not know it, but he turned and tossed in the bed; making guttural sounds from deep in his throat. Once he pointed into the corner of the room as if seeing something there.

But there was nothing there.

And thus, the night passed.

***

4

Ward woke the following day, puzzled by the dim quality of the light that barely made it through the gap in his curtains and equally puzzled by the fact that that he didn't feel in the slightest that he had enjoyed any sleep at all.

Drawing the curtains solved one problem at least: there was no sun, just horizon to horizon grey clouds that merged together into one depressing mass that had just about enough energy to drop a thin curtain of misty rain onto the dim street. In other words, a typical English May morning.

He did his usual routine of going through the material on his laptop. He looked through his e-mails finding the usual messages from unlikely females who wanted to share his bed even though they lived in Vladivostok but no messages from prospective employers (or real women for that matter). He opened his web browser and looked for vacancies in the software engineering department. He found a few and filled in his details. He hesitated as he always did when he came to the part about previous employment. His last real job (working behind the bar obviously didn't count) was receding farther and farther into the past. He filled in that section eventually after wondering whether or not they would contact his previous employer but decided that honesty was the best policy.

After that he found a few eggs and the last bit of bacon in the fridge and threw together a wholly unsatisfying lunch. While his stomach did its best in trying to digest his cooking, he decided that what he needed was a stiff drink. He glanced at his watch – it was after eleven; nothing unusual in imbibing a bit of the hard stuff at this hour.

Ward got his somewhat greasy raincoat out and took the stairs to the ground floor. The people in the foyer did not acknowledge him or even look at him. No-one acknowledged him. No surprise; they never did.

The streets were shiny with the soft rain as he walked as fast as he could through the mass of his fellow pedestrians who seemed to be taking a particular delight in impeding him this morning. Eventually the Admiral Benbow came into view and he hurried into it. As usual Betty was one of the people behind the bar, but he was acutely aware that she was regarding him with the same look that one gives to unpleasant substances discovered on one's sole.

'Morning Betty,' he said, as cheerfully as he could muster.

'And what's good about it?' was the frosty reply.

Ward decided to try and charm the woman.

'Every morning is a good one with you in it, Betty my one and only love.'

She said nothing.

Ward gave her his best smile, waited for the return kindly expression, didn't get it and so passed on to the business of the day.

'I'll have a double of the usual Betty, if you would be so kind.'

She glared at him.

'Oh no you won't.' With that she turned her head slightly and shouted 'Arthur! He's here again!'

The pub manager came out of wherever he had been having stopped whatever he'd been doing and came up to the bar directly opposite Ward.

'I thought I'd told you; you were barred Ward.'

Ward could remember no such thing. And there was something different about the manager.

Adopting a light tone, he said, 'Arthur! How long have you had that moustache? It suits you.'

Even as he said that Ward had another unpleasant feeling that something was awry: he had seen Arthur only yesterday and he hadn't had a moustache then; surely growing a tash wasn't an overnight affair?

Arthur hand went instinctively to the thin, sandy line of hair that stretched below his bulbous nose.

'What are you gabbling about Ward? I've had one for the last twenty years!'

A worm of cold fear began to climb Ward's spine; he knew that wasn't true. He hadn't known Arthur twenty years ago but, in the time that he had known him no hirsute appendage had ever appeared on his face; or on his scalp either, which was like a smooth pink egg.

Ward stood motionless, as the worm of fear completed its climb of his spinal column. He tried to speak but there was nothing.

Arthur seized on Ward's silence to issue his commandment.

'I told you last time not to ask for credit because a smack in the mouth sometimes offends. You'll get no more drink here unless I see some real money. Get out and stay out!'

Ward's head was swimming. Alcohol was no longer important: sanity

6

was. Without a word he turned and left.

Two hours later he was back at the table in his flat, staring down at his handgun.

This time there would be no mistake. He would do it slowly and carefully.

Slowly and carefully he lifted the weapon and placed it against his right temple.

There was a terrible noise, a feeling of intense heat and redness filled his vision.

Chapter Two

Dexter Ward knew that he should be dead, but he soon realised he wasn't. As his vision cleared, he became aware that he was looking down at a pair of hairy thighs, bedewed with little water droplets. A few seconds later he understood that they were his own thighs and that he had very recently been in contact with water because there was a garishly striped towel draped over his knees. At present he was sitting on what looked like a very expensive chaise-longue. He could not recall such an incongruous item in his down-market flat.

He lifted his vision to take in his surroundings and received yet another visceral shock: this was not his flat.

It was nothing like his flat; he was in a very large, very expensive-looking shower room with lots of marble and gold-coloured pipework. There was a pleasant smell of shower lotion and fragrant oils in the air and the air was warm and moist at precisely the correct temperature for human comfort.

He stopped his scanning of his surroundings abruptly because there was something else in the room which was exactly right for human comfort; or least male comfort.

In the large, two-person shower cubicle there was a naked woman; a woman vigorously towelling herself in a way that caused her breasts to oscillate in an extremely interesting manner. Ward stared at the breasts: they were exactly what his image of female perfection should be; not too large so that they were unable to support themselves against gravity; not too small so that they looked like overgrown goose-bumps. Like the Baby Bear's porridge, they were exactly right.

The naked vision turned in her towelling motion and looked right at him, giving him a flawless ivory smile as she did so. Ward continued to drink her in. She was so perfectly proportioned she could have been a drawing by Leonardo da Vinci. Viewed directly on she was simply stunning with tumbling blond locks caressing her shoulders as she continued the towelling, and, by the look of the damp curls in the pubic region, she was all natural.

She became aware of his intense stare and her smile turned into a somewhat puzzled expression.

'What?' she finally said, putting the towel behind her back and working it so vigorously that the golden orbs that adorned her thorax made incredible up-and-down gyrations.

Ward was so stunned that he found himself struck dumb with wonder. He could not move. He could not speak. If this was indeed madness it seemed to have its compensations.

The golden goddess came and sat beside him on the chaise. She smelled of sandalwood.

'Say something you old silly!' she murmured playfully, giving him a mock punch. 'Cat got your tongue?' At the word 'tongue' her hand briefly swept over his penis.

Words finally came to Ward. He had to say something; anything, otherwise he might never speak again!

'Uhh – who – who are you?' he finally managed to utter in a strange, strangulated voice.

The vision next to him frowned slightly, the very tiniest of lines appearing on the otherwise unblemished forehead.

'The same person I was when we came in here Dexter. Who do you think *you* are?'

Ward made small circular movements with his hands as he continued to stare at her.

'Humour me. I'm Dexter Ward. Who are you?'

The frown vanished and red lips parted to once again reveal the Hollywood teeth. 'Oh, I get it. One of your naughty games again.' She looked around conspiratorially. 'I'm Aoife. And I really shouldn't be here with you Mr. Ward. What if my husband finds out?'

Ward's heart leapt. Husband? What had this strange malady got him into this time?

'Husband?' he croaked, slightly drawing away from the woman – Aoife

9

– if that was her real name.

His tone must have convinced the woman that she was not in an erotic game and she leaned forward, getting so close to him that he could feel her breath.

'Snap out of it, Dexter!' she commanded, 'you're the husband. I'm Mrs Aoife Ward – unless you want me to be somebody else,' she added playfully, still not sure if they were really play-acting.

Ward relaxed slightly. He was married. How could he have forgotten that? And, more to the point, how could he forget that he was married to someone who looked like this? There had been a woman called Siobhan (what was it with him and women with Irish names?) but attractive though she had been she was a dandelion to this orchid.

No, no,' he finally said, 'Mrs. Dexter Ward will do just fine!' He heard the relief in his own voice and hoped that Aoife had not. He didn't want to spoil this moment. He needn't have worried; Aoife apparently was not. 'Good,' she purred and brushed his lips with the quickest of butterfly-wing kisses. Ward felt the swift touch of the softest of soft lips and suddenly realised he wanted more – a lot more. He hadn't been with a woman since God knew when and here he was, alone with the most alluring female he had ever seen – who thought she was his wife! Glancing down he realised that he too was naked – evidently he had just come out of the shower himself when – when whatever it was that had happened, had happened. He looked across the room at Aoife. There was a faint haze of steam in the room, but it was not enough to hide the fact that Aoife was now bending over towelling her knees with her back turned to him; her charms on display.

Instinct took over. If this was madness, then nothing mattered – not a damn thing!

He leapt up and, grabbing her from behind, closed his hands over the soft breasts, glorying in their spongy resilience. She cried out – apparently, he had been too rough. He didn't care. He spun her around and almost flung her onto the chaise. Her towel was thrown across the room as she lay on her back looking up at him in wonder. But not for long. Roughly he climbed on top of her and with one strong thrust was buried deep in her soft folds. This time she cried out much more loudly and earnestly than before. Ward ignored the cry and began pistoning back and forth, but he had been too long without a woman. In only a few seconds he gave a deep cry and emptied himself into her.

Then he lay there, quivering. And as he did so his lust-crazed mind began to clear. What had he done? This was a strange woman and he had raped her. Rape. It was an ugly word. And even if this stranger was in some crazy way his wife, even so …

He got off her, afraid for a few seconds to look at her. And when he did...

'You bastard!' she said, 'haven't you heard of foreplay! I was too dry. That hurt!'

I'm sorry,' Ward mumbled, looking down at the damp floor, 'I...'

Aoife stood up and walked over to retrieve her towel and began dabbing at her pubic region.

'And now I'll have to take another bloody shower!' She walked back to him. 'I don't get you Ward. We only had sex a few hours ago. Are you trying to prove something? That you're some kind of macho sex-machine? Grow up!'

Once again Ward began to mumble apologies but once again she cut him off. To his great relief she broke into a smile. 'Listen Macho Man. You don't have to prove anything with me. I'm happy with the way things are. Give this poor thing a well-earned rest' – and she reached down to give his flaccid penis a none-too-gentle tug.

'Yes, yes' said Ward, finally daring to look at her again.

She flung the towel onto a chair near the shower cubicle and began to walk towards it. Just before she entered, she looked back over her shoulder and said 'And don't forget now. No foreplay – No Aoife!'

**

The next morning Ward suddenly felt a sharp dig in his ribs as he lay there luxuriating in the warm softness of the double bed that took up a large proportion of the large bedroom.

A female voice hissed in his ear. 'Get up you slob! Don't you believe in working for a living?'

Ward looked at the bedside clock and could not believe the hour it showed. 7 AM? People got up at this time of the day? Then he remembered – he used to get up at a similar time when he had a job. Which must mean … he had a job.

A job. But with whom? And more importantly, where?

'I think I'll stay home today,' he mumbled turning on his side away from Aoife, 'feeling a bit under the weather.'

Aoife rolled on top of him and glared down. She was nude of course and her hair enveloped him in a golden curtain. Her nipples just touched his chest, gentle as the fall of a snowflake.

'Oh no you don't mister! You were full of beans yesterday as I recall – remember Mr. Love Machine? Off you go!'

Ward's mind raced. He'd already had to learn his wife's name by subterfuge – how could he tell her he didn't know where he worked? How many more questions before Aoife began to wonder if her husband had been replaced by a clone?

Ward had one desperate throw of the dice before admitting he wasn't Dexter Ward – that he was actually another man of the same name.

'You couldn't drive me in, could you darling? I'm really feeling a little off colour.'

Aoife was still on top of him. She looked to one side and said to the wall 'Dexter – you know I hate driving in London at this time of the day. Are you too good for the Tube or something?' She turned her head and glared down at him, moving infinitesimally lower so her breasts rested full on his chest. Ward's penis twitched slightly but he told himself: No – not now! Later! Later!

'Pretty please?' he finally managed to squeak.

She frowned again but finally said: 'OK. But you owe me big time. If it wasn't for your money, I wouldn't know why I do things for you.'

Ward's eyes narrowed slightly. Was that a joke? Was there a worm in the bud of this perfect marriage? No, of course not – it was just banter. No-one who actually thought that would be fool enough to say it.

To his relief Aoife finally got off him and started to get dressed.

'No time for a shower today thanks to you,' she muttered, in a voice loud enough for him to hear.

Ward lay on the bed, gazing in awe as this wonderful woman pulled on a pair of sheer black stockings. She caught his gaze and, lifting her head, demanded 'What in fuck's name is wrong with you Ward? You've seen this a million times before. And do you intend going to work in the nude?'

Ward suddenly realised that he didn't have time to ogle his wife and complied with the unspoken command.

Shortly afterwards they were winding their way through the rush-hour traffic. The car was sleek and powerful, and Aoife was an excellent, fearless driver, taking chances with oncoming cars that Ward would never have dared – and getting away with it every time.

Ward realised glumly that he could never have got to his workplace in time if he had been driving but Aoife seemed completely calm, which must mean that she had no doubt that they would soon be there.

And so it transpired.

Aoife swept the sports car into the car park in front of a steel and glass edifice that was topped with a massive sign which read Quantum Software Development. She waved a plastic rectangle which Ward assumed was a pass at the bored looking men in the security booth. Ward noticed with annoyance that they no longer looked quite so bored now that they had seen her.

'Out you get, Lover Boy. And Dexter…' She touched his shoulder gently.

'Yes?'

She gave a little twist to her face so the expression it showed was half annoyance, half concern.

'Try to be little bit normal when you get back, will you? You're starting to get creepy.'

Not half as creepy as I actually feel, Ward thought, but he said 'I'll be alright. Just working too hard, I guess.'

She laughed and her eyes seemed to sparkle.

'Working too hard? You? Get out before I kick you where it hurts!'

They exchanged a quick kiss and Ward duly got out. He watched the car shoot away at an impossible speed for the amount of traffic and he wondered to himself *What the hell have I done to deserve this? This woman is every man's dream. What have I done?*

It was then it came back to him that he hadn't done anything to deserve it. He had met the woman only yesterday and only had her word for it that she was his wife. And in his sex-crazed haze certain massive questions had been overlooked. Where was he? How had he got here? Why was he still Dexter Ward but a totally different Dexter Ward than he had been not very long ago?

13

Was this all a development of his illness and a complete hallucination? Was he actually at this moment clutching an empty whisky bottle in a dingy alleyway while the drizzle bedewed his torn clothes and dripped off his chin?

He shook his head. If he was going to wake up soon in an A&E Department then he would get the most out of this hallucination as he could. Aoife had certainly felt real yesterday, and she had shared his bed when the time came. Why worry?

Why worry? Well, there was still the little matter of doing a job he knew nothing about. He turned around to take a closer look at the steel and glass tower in which he apparently worked. He was unimpressed by the name of the company – sticking Quantum in a name was a cheap way of making a business seem modern and scientific. We shall see.

He strode into the spacious foyer and was walking past the reception desk when a man in uniform suddenly placed himself in front of him.

'Security pass, please sir.'

Ward decided to bluff it out.

'Come on, you know me. Dexter Ward.'

'That's as may be, but I still need your security pass, sir.'

Ward knew there was no point in prolonging the act.

'Sorry. I must have left it in my other jacket.'

The security man frowned making Ward feel like a small boy who had just been caught doing something very, very naughty.

'This is a serious breach, sir. I'll have to call your line manager.'

Ward's stomach lurched. If this goon asked him for his line manager's name, he was sunk. But Ward was apparently well known here. The guard spoke into a button on his lapel.

'Mr Jackson? Could you come down to the foyer please. I have to ask you to sign one of your people in.'

Ward waited nervously for Jackson to appear. The security guard ignored him. Finally, the lift doors opened and a spare man apparently in his late forties came out. As he approached, Ward had great difficulty in suppressing a guffaw for Jackson sported the most pointless comb-over that Ward had ever seen; there were so few hairs clinging desperately to his pink dome that Ward could actually count them.

'Ward, what's the meaning of this? Forgetting your security pass, what's

14

the matter with you man?'

'Well, it's the first time I've done it,' Ward replied, taking a lucky guess.

The guess was lucky, for Jackson nodded and said 'Yes alright. Everyone's entitled to one mistake I suppose. Alright Andrews, I'll sign him in.'

They crossed to the reception desk where Jackson scribbled something unintelligible on a pad and then he and Ward got into the lift.

'Are you OK, Ward?' Jackson demanded as the lift shot past floor after floor, 'Not having one of your funny periods again, are you?'

Ward groaned inwardly. Obviously, his doppelganger wasn't lucky in everything. He too must have Black Dog days. But as he thought that, he realised that he was approaching the high point of his cycle. He felt boundless energy and confidence flooding into his veins. He was going to ace this! He could do it! He seemed to have a good job and a good homelife and nothing was going to take it from him. Perhaps a passing angel had taken pity on him and changed the world to give him what he really deserved. A job he knew nothing about? – No problem!

'No boss,' he finally said, 'just a bit busy at home, you see.' And with that he gave a conspiratorial wink.

Jackson looked at him blankly for a split second and then gave out a surprisingly loud belly laugh.

'Yes, I've seen your wife Ward! I don't blame you! Just don't mix business and pleasure again – for a while at least!'

The lift doors sighed open and the two stepped out into a busy office where hordes of young men and women were busily bent over softly glowing computer monitors. No-one looked up. They were all too engrossed in the hieroglyphics on their screens.

Jackson pointed at an empty workstation. 'Well there you are. Better late than never. Get on with it.'

Ward sat down and despite his growing euphoria a tiny doubt nagged at his composure. Password? Password? How would he get the password to unlock his station? Then he laughed uproariously, causing several work colleagues to look around for an instant. It was retina controlled. He was sure that he and all the other Dexter Wards – wherever they were – must have the same retinal pattern.

And so it proved. The screen lit up and the words **Good Morning,**

Dexter Ward appeared reassuringly upon the screen. He looked into all the documents that he could find and quickly discovered that whatever it was that his alter-ego had been doing involved using a Front-End based on C++. He smiled sardonically; he was a bit rusty, but this was kindergarten stuff to an old pro like him. He would have to work late at the office for a few weeks to catch up to where the other Dexter Ward had left off, but in the blinding brilliance of his High Point, he knew he could do it. He had memorised the route from his place to here and knew he could get back by Tube tonight. But in the future, it would be in a magnificent roadster like Aoife's.

And when he could get back home at an early enough hour, he would show Aoife what being married to a Love Machine was really like.

Chapter Three

As the weeks passed Ward found his job easier and easier. The way his predecessor had structured the project was exactly the way he would done. (He gave wry smiles when that thought recurred to him during his short learning curve.) True, there had been a pronounced dip in his work output during his earlier days, but nothing had been said and he assumed they were giving him some leeway during a supposed down period. But the opposite was in fact the case. With each day his confidence soared until he became so good at his job that he began to consider it beneath him. Perhaps it was time he turned the tables and asked his boss for a quiet talk, during which he would suggest it was time for a promotion. After all there was no shortage of demand for people with his skills…

Aoife also no longer seemed to regard him as creepy. She had hinted every now and again that perhaps he could find some other hobby than vigorous sex for a while, but in the full flower of his confidence he had stowed that suggestion where it belonged. After all she had her interests – mainly it seemed, the gym where she was always to be found when he returned home to find the house unoccupied.

Then one early evening when he was feeling particularly proud of himself and nothing even slightly out of the ordinary had happened to him, there came a slight jolt in his idyllic existence. It had been a normal day at work. Everything had gone smoothly with the exception of a minor brown-out late in the afternoon. The office lights had dimmed and for an instant all the computer screens had flashed unrecognisable symbols overlain with complex moiré patterns. But everyone reported the same thing and it had only lasted a few seconds with no after-effects. The IT technicians confirmed it had not been a hacking attack. He had left the office and was walking across the outdoor car park to his own magnificent vehicle when he noticed an odd-looking motorbike with a strange silvery sheen parked nearby. What up-and-coming whizz-kid owns that beauty he idly wondered. Just then a figure stepped out in front of him.

Ward started and stared at the individual, looking for a gun or knife but he soon relaxed. The person was a small woman with a short bob of raven-black hair. There was nothing in the least sinister or alarming about her. She was neither pretty nor plain and had the general appearance of a small-town primary school teacher.

'Mr. Ward?' she enquired in a soft, quiet voice which somehow had an undercurrent of tension or worry under a melodious but completely unidentifiable accent.

He went to sweep past her. 'Sorry. Can't stop.'

She touched his arm as he brushed past. 'Mr. Ward, please stop. We need to talk – you're in great danger and we can help you. And you can help us.'

Ward felt suddenly angry. These charity collectors were becoming more and more intrusive and collaring him on the way to the car was simply too much. He glared down at the small woman. 'Listen and listen good. You've got your troubles – so have I. I don't see anyone collecting money for people like me. I just have to shrug my shoulders and get over my problems. I suggest you tell your overpaid do-gooders to try it. They might like it.'

With that he raised a finger to forbid the woman to speak again. She ignored the gesture.

'Mr. Ward, you don't understand. Please listen to me – I only have a limited amount of time outside the shield fields. It's a much bigger problem than you think. If you'll only allow me to talk to you for a short while.'

Ward shook his head without speaking and strode rapidly to his car. As he drove off, he glanced in his rear-view mirror. The woman was still standing there, staring at his disappearing vehicle.

As Ward drove away a strange thought began to climb up through the dark strata of his subconscious toward the light of the conscious mind. That woman seemed oddly familiar – but how could that be? He scanned the catalogue of recent events - no mean feat given recent developments – trying to find a pigeonhole in which that odd female's likeness could have been stored. He found nothing. And there was something else: the search for the mysterious female had somehow caused other visions to appear; visions of odd, gangly, elongated men who hid their faces.

Ward shook his head angrily. Just when he thought he had got his mental problems on the run these sort of things reared up to shake his self-belief. Sometimes he had the feeling that he was walking on a thin, brittle layer of sanity above a deep, dark lake of madness.

He realised that in his absorbed state he had overshot his house. With a muffled obscenity he reversed and then drove down the driveway to the door of his underground garage. The door recognised the vehicle and opened obediently.

He made his way to the lounge. He wanted a single malt and a talk with Aoife. No sex, just companionship and reassurance that all was well.

The room was empty. There was no sign that anyone had been there recently but there was a scribbled note on the drinks table, next to his Scotch.

'Darling,' he read, 'Gone to the gym tonight. I noticed my tummy was a millimetre wider than it was last week and I know how you like me to be slim and supple! Pour yourself a drink. You deserve it!'

Ward groaned. All he had wanted was a quiet night in with his wife; maybe watch a movie together on their giant screen TV. When did the bloody place close anyway – he hadn't heard of all-night gymnasia.

He pressed the button which made the TV emerge from the wall and turn itself on.

It started showing a report from the House of Commons where the political parties had once again failed to form a government. One brave MP was apparently arguing that the time-honoured voting system of the Single Transferable Vote should be replaced by a more modern system called First Past the Post. Ward watched it desultorily for a few minutes, not understanding a word or caring that he couldn't understand a word and then sent the TV back to its hidden lair.

He poured his drink. Then another.

He had gone to bed when Aoife came into the bedroom and, very quietly, slid into the bed next to the sleeping man.

***

Life slipped into a very comfortable groove for Ward. He had the inevitable downturn in his mood and outlook on life, the universe and everything in it but compared to previous ones, it was very mild. On the Richter Scale of downswings, it hardly rattled the teacups. The high, when it arrived, was on the other hand much higher. At times he felt quite godlike and more than capable of solving all the world's little problems. He did have a mild shock one day when Aoife, who was sitting next to him on the sofa, yawned loudly and raising her arms above her head enquired sweetly: 'That old gun of yours – why do you still keep it? You're not planning to do me in one day, are you?'

Until that moment Ward had not realised that his current incarnation was possessed of such an implement. He grinned weakly before thinking of something to say.

'No darling – it's just for security. The Have-Nots resent people like us who have worked damn hard to get where we are today and would like nothing more than to drag us down to their level. Well, if any low-life manages to get past our alarms the bastard will get a very nasty shock!'

Aoife smiled an entrancing smile and snuggled in closer.

'Dexter – what have I got to worry about with a man like you around?'

Ward nodded, while all the while his mind was racing. He hadn't known until then that he had a gun. Where was it? He could hardly claim to be the protector of the household if he didn't know a basic fact like that.

However, it wasn't long before Aoife was having one of her long sessions at the gym and Ward was alone in the house. He spent no little time searching before finally finding it in a drawer in one of the guest bedrooms. He immediately knew that this too was an unauthorised weapon which meant that this version of him must be prone to suicidal thoughts as well. He felt immediately sad for his predecessor (wherever he was) - here was a man who, almost literally, had everything and still could not escape the demons whispering in his ear that he was worthless and should end it all. He sat down on the bed and thought.

He had been so caught up in mastering his job and enjoying his time with Aoife that he had not thought for a long time about the central mystery – What the Hell was going on?

This wasn't his life; it bore no relation to the life he had been leading. He'd been down to where the Admiral Benbow should have been and there was a swish Korean restaurant there. On enquiring, he had been told that it had been there for years. Someone could remember that before the Koreans came it had been an Italian. But a down-market boozer? – No way!

He hadn't met anybody whom he had known before all this started; no one he could ask Do you recognise me? Do you know me? Do you know what the Hell is going on?

There remained the possibility that all this was happening within his brain. That something had flipped on the cellular level and that, in reality, he was in some isolation ward with white coated men standing over him, shaking their heads in pity.

Should he pursue the truth, whatever it was, or just enjoy the moment? He didn't know.

The question was too big for him – or anyone else, he suspected.

In the meantime, he had a good job, which his abilities would soon make better, and he had Aoife, who seemed to adore him. He certainly adored her: now that initial sexual frenzy had abated somewhat, he found himself looking at her and wondering what she saw in him.

She had noticed the stares a couple of times and laughed and said 'What?' in a playful manner. They had kissed and forgotten about it.

He remembered that a pop star had once talked about The Paradise Syndrome – the feeling of ennui that comes when all your dreams have come true. Well, that's what his feelings of disquiet must be – The Paradise Syndrome. He laughed to himself – all those people in the world, racked by hunger and disease; they didn't know the half of it!

***

The weeks wore on. Nothing unpleasant happened. Quite the contrary; he had finally forced his boss to give him some face time and had then made it clear that if his position wasn't adequately rewarded, he would walk. The boss had evidently been expecting this outcome for he gave in almost immediately. Ward became Head of Department with an increase in salary and, more importantly, lots of people younger than he to order around.

On one occasion, when walking to his new car, he thought he saw that odd little woman walking briskly towards him. It was raining so he could not be sure, but he increased his stride and drove off before she could get anywhere near him.

On that particular day, he had delegated large swathes of work to his

21

underlings so he could leave the office a lot earlier than usual. Being earlier, the traffic was lighter, so he arrived back home surprisingly soon. He thought he'd sneak in the house to give Aoife a lovely surprise. But as soon as he got in, he stopped dead in the hallway. He could hear voices; one was Aoife's sweet soprano but the other was a basso profundo with a distinct Teutonic accent. They were coming from the living room so Ward dropped his briefcase and marched straight in.

Aoife was on the sofa sitting close to a large man who had his back to Ward.

Ward could think of nothing to say other than 'Hello – what's this?', so he said it.

Aoife saw him over the man's burly shoulder and gave a smile which could have powered the National Grid for a month.

'Dexter! What are you doing back so soon? What a lovely surprise! You haven't met Gunter, have you?'

At that, the man on the sofa turned and stood up. He was wearing tight-fitting gym shorts and an even more tight-fitting sweatshirt which seemed to have been painted over bulging pectorals. He extended an arm the size of Ward's thigh and said in a strong German accent; 'Mr. Ward, it's good to meet you. What a lovely house you have here.'

Ward shook hands quickly, his hand disappearing entirely within Gunter's massive grasp.

'Yes, thank you,' he replied stiffly, 'Aoife and I like it here.'

Aoife came around Gunter's side so she could actually see her husband.

'You've heard me talk of Gunter, Dexter darling. He's my personal trainer.'

Ward's eyes narrowed. Those words had an achingly familiar ring. The particular scenario that haunted him flashed briefly across his mind, but he drove it away: that had happened to a different Dexter Ward; a loser, a near down-and-out; a man with nothing to live for. That Dexter Ward was gone; gone into an eldritch labyrinth of metaphysical mystery. He was not him.

'Gunter, yes of course,' he replied, unconsciously lowering his voice a semitone or two, 'yes. You're working my wife' (was there a slight emphasis on that phrase?) 'very hard I understand.'

Gunter grinned, revealing tombstone teeth that were almost as brilliant as Aoife's. 'I don't have to work your wife very hard, Mr. Ward. She is very flexible. Very ah - supple - I think that is the correct word, is it not?'

'Indeed,' Ward said stonily, wishing this inane conversation would end soon. He decided to end it.

'Well Mr. – uh – '

The slab of a man grinned again. 'I feel we are friends, Mr. Ward. Just call me Gunter.'

'Well, Gunter, it has been an unexpected pleasure meeting you here in my home but no doubt you are a very busy man. Probably almost as busy as I am.'

Gunter nodded. 'I am Mr. Ward – or may I call you Dexter?'

'Yes,' Ward said at last, but through gritted teeth.

'Well Dexter, it has been very - very pleasant, I believe is the phrase - to see you here, in your wonderful house. Perhaps we three could go out for a drink some evening. There are many excellent wine bars around here and there are many German wines that I would like to introduce to you.'

'That would be splendid,' Ward said slowly, thinking that if this man didn't go soon, he would explode. 'Absolutely – splendid.'

'Excellent,' Gunter replied, apparently oblivious to Ward's rising tension. He turned briefly to Ward's wife. 'Now Aoife, I look forward to go through that new exercise programme with you tomorrow. You said you wanted something more demanding, I believe.'

'Yes, I did, didn't I?' Aoife beamed, with eyes that seemed to sparkle. 'Auf wiedersehen, Gunter.'

Gunter nodded good-naturedly and turning to Ward smiled and said, 'And to you Dexter, au revoir.'

When Gunter had finally gone Ward exploded.

'What do you mean bringing that lunk into my house! Is this what you get up to while I'm working my bollocks off in that bloody office!'

Aoife sat elegantly in the nearest armchair and looked up at Ward under blue-tinted eyelids with lips in an arch semi-smile.

'*Our* house, darling. And what does this childish exhibition mean? I always thought my husband was a strong, stable man, secure in his skin, happy with his sexuality.'

'I am,' spluttered Ward, conscious that he was somehow losing the moral high ground.

23

Aoife's semi-smile became a sweet, enticing whole smile. 'Darling, you mustn't be jealous like this. It's just silly, and frankly, a little demeaning coming from a grown man. You have everything Dexter – a marvellous job, a marvellous house – why have a hissy fit over a muscle-bound dimwit like Gunter? You've got all those wonderful things and,' she got up from the armchair and sidled up to him, placing her hands on his shoulders and bringing her lips nanometres from his, 'you've got me!'

The rest of the discussion was accomplished without words.

Chapter Four

Ward's life flowed along very pleasantly. He had not been in a position of authority over others for some considerable time and he liked it. More and more he was the Go-To Guy for when there was a problem that the youngsters couldn't handle. The upper echelons had noticed, and Ward knew that another promotion was more or less inevitable.

He no longer needed to work late but he felt guilty about turning up early and unannounced at the house. It would be obvious that he was checking up on Aoife and her little lecture to him was still raw. He did not want to appear to be an insecure saddo; those days were gone.

One day he had easily finished his work allocation and he had trained his staff so well that it didn't look like anyone would be asking him any questions. He decided he would NOT go home early; he would show that he was a secure, confident executive who had everything under control.

There was a new wine bar not far from his house. He would park near his home but not put the car away. He would then walk to the wine bar and see if he could pick up some knowledge of the more obscure German wines; enough to put Gunter in his place, if ever he were unfortunate enough to meet that gentleman again. Then if he should end up over the limit it would be a simple matter to carefully drive the car into his garage.

His mind made up, he put his fingers to the keyboard in order to close his workstation down. As he did so, all the lights in his room dimmed slightly and became yellowish. The HTML on his screen disappeared as it flashed up unusual symbols, overlain with shifting moiré patterns. He was able to get a better glimpse of the symbols this time, but they remained impenetrable: they were not Chinese characters, or Cyrillic or Arabic. Ward's knowledge of mathematics was limited but they did not appear to be mathematical symbols either. Then the lights flared up into their normal white brilliance and the symbols were gone.

There was a brief hubbub in the room.

'There it goes again!'

'What the hell was that?'

'Are they sure it's not a virus?'

Nothing else happened and the staff lost interest. So did Ward. Putting his plan into action he bade good evening to his slightly surprised people and left the office.

Autumn was well advanced, and twilight was already in evidence as Ward drove past his house. There were no other cars parked directly outside it.

Good.

He spent some time in the wine bar, imbibing enough to strike up conversations with total strangers, but the time finally arrived for him to go home. By now the outside world was quite dark and chilly enough for Ward to regret not wearing an overcoat. He looked around for a few moments, fearing that he had forgotten where the car was or that it had been stolen but eventually, he spotted it at the end of the street.

The shadows were deep in the street; the wine bar was the only public establishment on it. As he briskly walked along, he noticed one shadow at the corner of a large building seemed darker than the others.

And then it moved.

As it moved it took on the form of a tall, gangling man with what seemed to be very long arms. The face was hidden beneath a tightly wrapped scarf and the top of the head was covered by a close-fitting cap. Only the eyes were visible, and they seemed to momentarily catch the light with a greenish glow, like a cat caught in headlights.

There came a voice; thin, whispery and somehow laboured, as if speaking caused the figure some considerable effort.

'Ward. We need to speak with you. You can help us.'

For a second or so Ward was unable to move as the man bore down on him; as he approached Ward reckoned the stranger was about two metres tall.

Then Ward ran.

He ran to the car and without looking in the rear-view mirror drove to his house.

He hurriedly locked the door behind him and went to the window, pulling the curtain to half cover him.

He scanned the dark street.

Nothing.

No tall, thin shape was there.

He sat down heavily and placed his head in his hands.

What was that! It was a man but – but – somehow there was something unpleasantly unusual, something unnatural.

Not just the extreme height but the proportions of the body.

They were – wrong.

He began to shiver. He felt that the thin crust of sanity over the deep lake of madness was beginning to crack. He had adjusted to his new life and no longer asked questions about how he had got here; how it had happened. He was content to make his way in this world as if it were the only one he had ever known. He did not want to be reminded of the mysteries that enfolded him.

But there were mysteries out there.

And they wanted a word with him.

He heard a noise behind him and whirled around, giving a small sigh of relief when he saw that it was Aoife.

'What in hell's name are you up to Dexter?' she demanded. 'Why are you trying to pull the curtain down on top of you?'

Relief made Ward gabble somewhat. 'I had – I met- some mugger came up to me – I…'

'You better make yourself a drink. No – wait. By the smell of you, you've already had too much.'

She guided Ward to a nearby sofa and sat down beside him.

'My, you have had a fright, haven't you?' She placed scarlet-tipped fingers on his chest. 'I can feel your little heart going thumpety-thump!'

He pushed the hand away angrily and stared into the gloom, ignoring his wife.

Something was terribly wrong – but what?

Two people, two very different people, had approached him, talking in strange accents, both saying that he could help them.

How could he help total strangers?

He looked back at Aoife; her face inscrutable in the semi-darkness.

27

Could she help him?

Perhaps no-one could.

Something was wrong; very wrong.

***

It was a very subdued Ward that went to the office the following day. He spent some time away from his work files, scanning the local news websites for a mention, however brief, of tall, ungainly foreigners, but there were none. When he finally started work, he soon realised that he had made several elementary errors and had to start all over again.

He became aware from catching the odd look from his boss that the automatic promotion he had been sure of was slipping from his grasp.

The day dragged on. He half-waited for the lights to dim and unknown symbols to dance across the screen. He had remembered that on both of the occasions that strangers had approached him asking for help that they had been preceded by that odd phenomenon.

He took to leaving early and going straight home; a routine which Aoife had found amusing at first but an amusement that slowly morphed into annoyance.

Finally, she said 'Are you sure you haven't been sacked Dexter? You're not one of those men who pretend to be going to work but actually spend all day in the library, are you?'

'Don't you like having your husband around,' he had snapped back, 'haven't you got a new workout to perfect with Gunter?'

An unwise rejoinder as it turned out, as she then began to spend even more time at the gym. Dexter began to wonder if he was actually still a married man and suddenly realised that his long High Point had come to a train-wreck of an end.

Several times he went to the drawer and looked down at the handgun. Once he took it out, savouring its cold heaviness in his hand. Was not oblivion preferable to this insidious insanity that was gradually spreading through his brain like some obscene slime-mould?

Why continue existing when there was no guarantee that his mind would not start spewing out worse and worse episodes of delirium? In all probability there was no Aoife, no office, no job, no sanity, just crawling, red-eyed madness, dribbling sick saliva from its jaws.

He vowed that if that woman came up to him again, he would grab her

28

and demand that she explained what this craziness was all about, even if he had to beat it out of her. Several times he looked around while opening his car door but there was no woman and, thank God, no tall, ungainly man either.

And then, one day, it happened again.

The lights dimmed and went yellowish. Ward immediately turned his gaze to his computer screen, staring at the symbols that appeared. They were only visible momentarily, but Ward was sure they were not the same ones he had seen during the previous incident. What did that mean? He would find out, he grimly assured himself.

Nothing happened that day but as he was leaving the office the next day, he espied the strange woman bearing down on him. He held his ground despite his heart beginning to flutter. It ends here! he told himself.

As the woman came within hailing distance, he studied her closely. Ward was no expert on women's attire, but he knew that she was dressed oddly with bulbous purplish leggings and a translucent green blouse over which she had a kind of satchel, which by the way it hardly swung appeared to be very heavy. She looked extremely underdressed for the time of year.

'Mr. Ward!' she called as she came near.

That's me,' Ward growled. This person looked more normal than the shadowy figure he had seen some weeks earlier, but he did not know if she was friend or foe.

She stopped a metre away looking up at him with what seemed to be an imploring expression.

'Mr. Ward – I have to talk with you.'

'I'm listening,' Ward replied stonily – that accent - was it Spanish?

'Thank you, thank you,' she answered effusively, 'I – '

She stopped. Something had rung in the satchel. She looked at it with a mixture of annoyance and apprehension.

'Excuse me Mr. Ward I have to check the Higgs.'

Ward stood motionless, thinking Higgs? Isn't he a character in Dickens? *David Copperfield* or *Oliver Twist*?

She reached into the satchel and took out a small silvery rectangular object which she touched in several places in quick succession. Her face was then lit up by a reddish glow as she looked at something on the side hidden from Ward.

'Oh, it's alright. False alarm.' She put the object away and looked back at Ward.

'I have a lot to say to you Mr. Ward I hope you have time.'

'I'm waiting,' was Ward's cold rejoinder. 'You'd better hurry up before I call security. How did you get onto the premises in any case?'

She ignored that and looked around furtively.

'I don't know how much time I have today. The Primans are near and they are interfering with my occupation of this probability.'

Ward once again felt dumbfounded. She had spoken an English sentence but as before it had made no sense. *Priman? Wasn't that a kind of stove that outdoor types took with them when they went camping?*

'We can talk in my car,' he finally said, turning and pointing. As he did so there was a sudden mechanical purring noise as if a powerful, finely-tuned engine had just turned on.

He turned back and his blood ran cold.

She was gone.

***

Ward sat in his armchair at home feeling tired, dispirited and totally defeated.

Nothing made much sense and as time rushed by, it was making less and less sense.

He felt completely drained with as much energy as a stranded jellyfish. Aoife had been wonderful; she had fussed around him and made a special effort to cook, which was remarkable for a woman whose normal idea of preparing a meal was picking up her mobile phone. When Ward finally finished her offering, he was forced to admit it wasn't too bad at all.

She led him to the armchair and helped him sink into it.

'There Dexter darling you've had a terrible day. I know how hard you work at that place to get us all these nice things. Don't think I don't appreciate it. Here.' She placed a tumbler of whisky in his hand and shushed his protestations that he didn't want one just yet.

'Don't be silly; you've earned it, if anybody has. Relax. I'll leave you alone for a bit while I put the dishwasher on.'

Dexter took his liquor neat and without ice. She had given him a generous measure and he sipped it slowly while he ran over the seemingly unending succession of strange things that were happening to him.

Gradually a terrible weariness came over him and he just managed to put the tumbler on the nearby table before falling into a deep, dreamless sleep.

He awoke with a start having no idea how much time had passed. He began to rise up out of the chair but found he could not.

Someone had tied him to the chair. He wriggled around, trying, more and more desperately, to break free.

'Aoife!' he eventually cried, 'Untie me! I'm too tired for these silly games.'

Aoife came into the room.

She was wearing latex gloves and in one gloved hand she had Ward's gun.

Ward got even more angry. 'Aoife stop it! I told you I'm too bloody tired!'

Aoife's face was as emotionless as if it had been carved from marble.

'You won't have to worry about being too tired. Or having to go to that terrible office you hate. I'm going to solve all your problems. With this.' And she lifted the gun.

Ward suddenly realised that he was not an unenthusiastic player in a sex game.

'What – what? You're going to kill me? Why? After all I've done for you!'

Aoife gave a smile; the sort of smile a striking Black Mamba could show to its prey; if such a thing were possible.

'Because I hate you. I hate your stupid moods and your self-pity; how you moan about the world and how you'd be better off dead because nobody loves you. And the funny thing is – you're right. Nobody loves you and you would be better off dead.'

Ward finally realised the enormity of his situation. This she-devil was going to kill him.

He began pulling at the knots that held his arms behind the chair-back. They had not been tied very professionally. He could get them off if he had enough time!

Aoife continued her unemotional delivery. There was no anger; no contempt – nothing.

'You're a sad man Ward. When you have your bad days – that's the real you. I'll get the house, your capital – everything. Gunter and I have already

31

worked out what we're going to do with it.'

'Gunter?' Ward gasped – but somehow that name did not come as a complete shock. He continued working at the knots – he could do it!

Aoife came nearer to him and for the first time there was a hint of emotion in her voice.

'When I told Gunter how you raped me, he was going to come around and tear you to pieces with his bare hands. And he could have done it too. But I said – not yet; we're not ready. I saved your life. And now I'm going to take it.'

Ward knew that he only needed a few more seconds to break free and then he would knock this she-devil to the floor, sit on her and tear her stinking windpipe out!

One more second!

Aoife placed the muzzle against his right temple.

'Suicide. Very sad – but in your state – inevitable really. Goodbye Ward.'

There was a terrible noise and a feeling of intense heat.

Chapter Five

Although Ward knew he was not dead, for a few moments he thought he might be in Hell. He was face down on something soft while waves of heat broke over him as if he was lying too close to a mighty oven. Slowly he turned his head and even more slowly opened his eyes, afraid of what he might see.

There were no devils with pitchforks. Instead there was a strip of yellowish vegetation and what might be a distant view of the sea on the horizon and above that a pale blue sky.

He raised himself so he was on hands and knees, feeling the roasting temperatures washing over him with lingering tongues of insidious heat that wrapped themselves around him in bands of near pain.

He stood up at last. He was dressed only in a loincloth and rope sandals. There was a cloth bag at his feet with lumpy objects inside. He looked around seeing a parched yellow landscape, similar in general appearance to nature videos he had seen of the African veldt. There were only a few stumpy trees; apart from that, the land seemed to be a single monotonous stretch of yellow grass. And the heat! Surely this was Africa!

What was this version of Dexter Ward doing in Africa? His earlier exemplars had shown no interest in that continent or any other form of exotic travel. And if he had gone there for work why was he dressed so wretchedly?

He picked up the bag and looked inside, almost instantly regretting his actions. There were four rabbits inside; one had been skinned and was now covered in flies.

Good God! he thought, send me back! I'll take my chances with Gunter!

What was he doing in this Godforsaken place, dressed like some survivor of a shipwreck?

He took one last look at the bag of rabbits and decided to leave it where it lay – although he was hungry, there must be something better to eat somewhere.

Two hours later, he was regretting his decision. He had trudged through the unending grass in the unending heat and seen nothing. Perhaps the bag would still be there. But, raw rabbit? How he could make a fire with no implements? He was a city boy; he had seen the survival programmes on TV where ingenious folk had lived off the land (being filmed all the time, of course) but he had thanked his lucky stars that he was not one of them and changed the channel to something else. But now his rumbling stomach told him he was in big trouble again and this time he could see no way out.

He crested a small ridge and found himself looking down on a group of ruined buildings, lying in a shallow valley. Although ruined, the buildings might give him some indication of where he could find civilisation and help.

Tired, hungry and covered in glistening sweat he made his laborious way down the side of the ridge. The poorly made sandals gave him little protection from the stony ground, and he had exhausted his vocabulary of expletives by the time he reached the pile of stones that marked the beginning of the group of buildings.

A gate hung by one hinge from a post that had once been painted white, if the few flakes that clung to the rotten wood were a clue to the past. Ward stopped, for there was a sign hanging down from one of the horizontal bars with whatever was written on the other side out of view. He turned it over and stood staring at the faint words that had been painted on the reverse.

Meadowcroft Farm.

That was a strange name for a building in Africa, he thought – it seemed more suited to a rural idyll in England's green and pleasant land, with sturdy farming-folk quaffing flagons of cider after bringing in the harvest. But Africa?

He walked into the nearest of the ruined buildings; stepping very gingerly over vicious shards of glass and tin cans with serrated lids still attached. There were empty wooden boxes and shredded remnants of what might once have been cardboard boxes. Inside one of the wooden boxes were a few sheets of faded paper lying under several layers of ochre dust. Ward took them out very carefully in case they crumbled into the same dust that covered them and blew the coating away. The text and picture on the top sheet had faded into almost total illegibility but by holding it obliquely and away from the sun he was just able to make out the title.

It was *Wilderness Survival*. The headline was: *New survival advice from* the *English Government*.

Ward was not the outdoor type, but he hadn't heard there was a need for survival advice from any government, least of all one apparently speaking for England. And what was it doing in a ruined English-style farmhouse in the heart of Africa?

It was then he heard movement in the room next to the one he was standing in. He stood rigid, awaiting whatever it was to reveal itself. A warthog? A leopard?

Then through the jagged gap that had once been a doorway two dangerous-looking men came into the room. They were dressed similarly to Ward, but their clothes were in slightly better condition. Both had straggly beards which looked like the kind that men develop when they don't really want beards but for some reason are unable to shave.

And one had a shotgun, pointed directly at Ward's genitals.

'You'd better explain what you're doing here fella,' the one with the shotgun said, in an unmistakeable Six Counties accent.

Ward was unable to speak for some seconds. It was a very good question – what was he doing here on the African savannah instead of doing complex coding in Quantum Software Development?

'I'm not doing anything,' he finally managed to articulate, 'Look – I'm hungry – have you got any food?'

The two men looked briefly at each other and Ward found he didn't like the type of look that they had just exchanged.

The other man, who had an even more straggly, greasier beard than the one with the shotgun, approached Ward, taking care not to get between Ward and the weapon.

'There's nothing to eat around here,' he said and then suddenly grinned, revealing the rotten stumps of a few surviving teeth, 'Except you maybe.'

If it had been possible for Ward's blood to run cold in that inferno, it would have done so.

Once again, he appeared to be in a life-or-death situation and this time without any apparent way of escape. Automatically he began to back out the way he had come, all the while keeping a desperate eye on the two men. He hadn't gone far when he felt something hard and very, very sharp digging in the small of his back. Automatically he stopped and raised his hands in surrender.

'Look,' he said, not turning around, 'I've done nothing. Who are you? What do you want?'

The person who had put the point of a knife in his back came around him and gave another black-stumped grin. It was a thin youth of about sixteen.

'He's got a bit of meat on him, dad,' he said and prodded Ward's belly with the knife point.

The man with the shotgun came nearer, raising the shotgun muzzle to navel level as he did so.

'We've got no fucking food fat boy. Have you? Come up with something quick cos we got no room for strangers around here.'

Ward suddenly thought about the rabbits. Why, oh why, had he left them there? Could they save him?

'I've got rabbits!' he blurted. Shotgun Man looked unimpressed.

'Where? In here?' and he pushed the barrels into the soft flesh of Ward's belly.

'No, no, I stored them some place near here. It's about two hours away.'

'Where?'

Ward explained, thinking *Please, please, let them be still there*!

The second man glanced at Shotgun Man and then at the youth. 'That's not two hours from here. Karl, you go get 'em.'

'OK dad,' the youth replied and was gone almost immediately. Ward watched him go – how could he move so fast in this heat?

'Karl won't be long,' the youth's father said, 'while we're waiting tell us why you've muscled in on our territory.' He and the other sat down on the nearest pieces of horizontal masonry.

'Yeah, do that,' Shotgun Man said, with a twisted smile, 'and don't say

36

anything that might annoy us.'

Ward also sat down. *And where do I begin?* he thought, *In my flat? In the Admiral Benbow? Having sex with Aoife? Which completely unbelievable part of my insane past do I beguile them with?*

In the end he simply said: 'I didn't know this was your territory. I'm sorry.' He thought somewhere in his whirling mind that that must be the truth; the original Ward must be a newcomer to this area or this scenario would already have happened.

Karl's father shrugged and looked at the other man.

'Funny that's what they all say – before we kill them.'

Shotgun Man laughed loudly.

Time passed achingly slowly. Nobody said anything else. The two men looked steadily at Ward who tried to match their stares, found he couldn't and ended up staring at his dirty feet in the tatty sandals.

Then there was a scrabbling sound behind him, and Karl came into view and – joy of joys – he was holding the rabbit bag!

'There's four of 'em in here!' the youth yelled, apparently in genuine excitement.

Shotgun Man looked at Ward with what appeared to be dawning respect.

'Four rabbits. You must be good mate.'

Karl's father nodded.

Ward relaxed slightly. Thank God his predecessor had been good at hunting.

'Yes, I am,' he said, forcing a smile, 'I can be of use to you.'

The first man lowered the shotgun and broke it so it could not be fired accidentally.

'OK. We'll try you out. Let's go to the camp.'

As they all rose to their feet Ward could not help blurting out: 'Guys – can you tell me what part of Africa this is?'

The two men exchanged puzzled glances and then Karl's father turned back to Ward.

'Are you trying to be fucking funny pal?'

'No' said Ward, 'I've had a bang on the head, see. What part is this?'

Shotgun Man said: 'Norfolk.'

***

37

The camp was just that; some poorly constructed shelters made of old logs and ferns; others equally basic, constructed from bits of tarpaulin and rotting planks.

Any tribe used to life in the wild could have done a hundred times better.

It had been evening when they arrived, and a slightly cool breeze was coming in off the nearby sea. Ward's rabbits were quickly cooked by some undernourished-looking women and Ward was even allowed a few pieces.

Trying to keep his gorge from rising as he chewed the tough stringy meat, he briefly thought of the last meal he had had with Aoife. He had thought it good then: if he could have it now it would be the veritable Food of the Gods! There were a few wrinkled berries to go with the meat; clearly the tribe had some empirical understanding of the need for Vitamin C even though Ward suspected they all were dangerously close to developing scurvy.

After the last of the meal had been washed down with bitter tasting, luke-warm water he was approached by the first of the men he had encountered, thankfully no longer bearing the shotgun.

'The Professor wants a word with you,' he said and pointed to the best of the shelters; although best was an extremely relative term in the circumstances.

Ward ducked his head and went into the acrid smelling gloom of the Professor's dwelling. He didn't recognise the smell at first but then a memory came back – tobacco!

In the gloom he finally espied a figure sitting cross-legged on the floor, or rather, ground.

'Come in Mister …?' the figure said.

Ward introduced himself and sat down expectantly.

As far as he could see the Professor was a lean man in his sixties with a mane of white hair and a similarly white, untrimmed beard.

'I am glad to see you are not one of the Weird Ones,' the professor observed.

Depends what you mean by 'weird' Ward thought, but he answered 'No, definitely not.' Then a second later he thought *Weird Ones?*

'I hear you've had a bang on the head and are not sure where you are.'

'Yes, yes,' Ward replied excitedly. *Answers at last?*

'Well,' the Professor began, 'this is the ancient county of Norfolk in the proud and splendid Kingdom of England.'

Ward could not help shaking his head. 'But the heat. The dryness. Why is everything so hot?'

The Professor stared at Ward for a few seconds as if he had asked if water was really wet. Then, finally accepting that the latter was serious, he began to explain, speaking as if he were addressing a particularly afflicted child.

'It was climate change of course. We have been burning fossil fuels for centuries now, in fact ever since the Industrial Revolution began in the early 1700s.'

In the reeking gloom, Ward frowned slightly. That couldn't be right: he was no historian, but he was sure the Industrial Revolution hadn't started until the early Nineteenth century. The Professor's dates seemed to be at least fifty years too early. He decided not to challenge his new host and pressed on: 'So what happened?'

'The climate changed, of course, slowly at first so many people denied it was happening or that it was just a natural fluctuation but gradually the changes picked up speed and when most people believed it was too late. The Tropics became too hot for human life and coastal areas were lost to the sea. I'm told by those few people who are older than me that Norfolk is only half the size it used to be. And so, the age of mass migrations began. Most of the people who live in England now are of African descent. They still believe in Allah despite all that has happened apparently.'

Ward sat back on his haunches. He had heard of Climate Change of course but he had too many problems going on in his own head to think much about it, but one thing he was sure of: it had not been as bad as this when he had sat down in his flat that fateful evening. And yet, if he assumed the Professor was right about the early date of industrial development and that the whole mess had been caused by human irresponsibility then this was the world one should expect.

Something else hit him as the Professor looked on in kindly puzzlement; every time he had woken up as a different Ward, things had been changed. At first, they had been very minor, such as Arthur's moustache but the differences had been amplifying. Where he was now had very little resemblance to where he had started which meant that if it happened again, he would be even more disconnected from his origin. And it appeared he was on a one-way highway into greater and greater weirdness.

And he had thought he had had problems before!

Chapter Six

Ward fitted in fairly well into the group (or tribe as he couldn't help thinking of them). He had visited Norfolk on a number of occasions and he began to recognise features in the landscape now that he no longer saw it as an African savannah, but apart from the heat and the lack of greenery there was another big difference: the sea was much, much closer than it should be.

His body appeared to have retained some muscle memory of its previous hunting ability and it wasn't long before he had caught some feral cats which made a welcome addition to the distinctly limited menu options in the camp.

He learned that the Shotgun Man was Liam, and Karl's father was Dave. Both had known no other way of life than what they had now and seemed basically content with it. Both had looked askance at Ward when he had made faltering attempts to explain what his own world was like and he decided that he was pushing the *Bang on the Head* excuse too far and dropped the subject, never to mention it again.

He noticed a few other things as well: despite being called Fat Boy earlier on, his body was in his own opinion at least, distinctly lean. And it was covered with many scars. Add to that the fact that this body seemed to have arthritis in the knees and one question was answered: these rebirths he was experiencing could not mean he was suddenly immortal. The new bodies - if that's what they were – had signs of degeneration. To put it another way; he was not getting any younger.

The hunting parties that he was now a regular member of were made up of all the men young enough to go out into the wild and that was the majority of them for there was only one other man apart from the Professor who was in his sixties.

41

The grasslands were not teeming with life; most of the animals were hares and rabbits plus feral cats and dogs. There were many parakeets flittering around from bush to bush, but they remained out of reach. The Wilderness Survival magazine was obviously from an earlier time when agriculture had still been possible.

Occasionally they would see other bands in the distance, once close enough to hear them speaking in a language that resembled Arabic, but the groups tended to avoid each other because, with resources being so limited, contact was almost always followed by violence.

However, Ward could easily see that his own band were the only ones that resembled the native English he had known before. Why this group had not gone north, he had no idea except perhaps with the island of Britain not being particularly large, the north probably was not that much different from the south. Perhaps civilised life hung on in Iceland or Arctic Norway. He would never know for the people of Norfolk no longer possessed any other means of transportation than their legs.

He spent as much time as he could with the Professor who was obviously flattered to speak to someone who actually believed what he was saying. Ward learned much from the man about the history of this new world; he learned that there had been no World Wars – just a lot of smallish ones. This existence was clearly no more peaceful than the last. There was one big difference: atomic weapons and hence atomic energy had not been discovered. There had been no nuclear reactors which might have slowed the build-up of greenhouse gases; just endless burning of coal and petroleum.

On one occasion he remembered a phrase the Professor had used during their first encounter: Weird Ones. Ward could not think what the words could refer to in Hothouse Norfolk, so he probed further during his usual evening talks with the man.

'These Weird Ones you mentioned, Professor. Exactly why do you call them that?'

The old man looked at Ward from under eyebrows that resembled furry white caterpillars stuck to his face.

'They don't look like us.'

'Why is that? Are they a different colour? – I've seen a lot of black people around here.'

'No – they are tall, very tall. And they move in a different way as if they are walking through water.'

Ward went rigid and every muscle seemed to tense.

No, no, no! he thought, *Not here, please! They are following me! But how? How?*

The Professor noticed his sudden tension and silence.

'Ward, what is it? Do you know something about the Weird Ones?'

Ward replied slowly and carefully; he could not give too many details or be thought insane.

'I saw one once – a long time ago. He wanted to talk to me. That's all.'

The Professor looked unconvinced, but he did not press the issue.

'Well I think we've spoken enough for one night. I like you Ward; you seem more intelligent than the other men here. They can't see further than the next rabbit. But you talk as if you have seen a wider world. I like that.'

Ward nodded in acceptance of the compliment, but he thought to himself: *The wider world? You don't know the half of it!*

***

Ward woke after a troubled night in which the crazy events of his recent past marched through his brain in a jumbled phantasmagoria of madness. Whatever was tormenting him had obviously not finished its cruel play and like a cat was letting him think he had escaped and then, extending its claws, dragging him back in for more suffering.

Each time he had awoken from apparent death he had found himself in a worse situation than before; in the previous versions he had suffered alone, now he was a helpless nonentity trapped like millions of others in a ruined world; ruined beyond all hope of redemption. Was some insane deity playing with him; some deity to whom human suffering was but a trivial joke, much as a small boy might laugh as he brought ruin upon an ants' nest?

Ward's distracted senses finally registered that the relative coolness of the night was over, and that yellowish light was beginning to infiltrate into the hut he shared with five other men. This day, like every other day, would be one for hunting; if the search for small inoffensive mammals could be dignified with such a grandiose term.

Liam pushed the tarpaulin aside and stuck his head into the foetid gloom.

'Come on Ward you bastard,' he yelled, 'time to be up and about!'

43

Ward noticed that the derogatory term was now used in matey way; he had been accepted into the tribe. He was still too low in the hierarchy to have a woman of his own, but he was sure that before long he would be offered a share in one; as for a woman for his personal use – that was way above his pay grade.

The men assembled in what could generously be described as the centre of the encampment before being given their orders; the groups would split into two main bands – one heading inland, the other heading for the coast. Ward felt a small sense of relief when he heard that he was in the coastal patrol; he knew that the warm sea was not too distant; even for arthritic knees. He checked his equipment to make sure that there could be no loss of face in front of his compatriots; he didn't know how deep their new-found respect for him really was. Catch bag: Check. Throwing stick: Check. Water flask: Check. Only Liam carried a weapon even though Ward was beginning to wonder if it actually did anything; he had never seen it fired.

Liam and Dave were in his group along with two others of about the same rank as Ward, but they had little to say and what they did say was always ignored so Ward gave his attention to Dave and Liam.

Dave, he learned previously, had great hopes for Karl. He had seen that the boy was intelligent and quick to learn; maybe one day he would become leader of the tribe, or maybe strike out on his own and found a new tribe.

As they trudged through the knee-high grass Ward tried to strike up a conversation with Dave. Although he no longer tried to explain his own circumstances he was interested in Dave's view of the world and what the future might hold.

'So, do you believe the Professor when he says the world wasn't always this hot?'

Dave shrugged. 'I don't know; the bugger says a lot of crazy things; things you can't believe. Like he says in very cold times water used to turn into a stone you could walk on. Hah! Anyway, what does it matter? Things are what they are and they're a lot worse overseas; that's why we've got all these black guys coming in. I tried talking to one before I killed him once and he talked some shit about dust storms and heat that killed you if you stood out in the sun at midday.'

Ward mused silently over that one. Dave might not believe in killing heat, but he did. And if what the Professor had said was true: it was coming this way.

They walked on. In the distance heat hazes caused the air to ripple and flow with the appearance of distant water.

'What about food,' Ward continued after a long gap, 'There's never enough to eat. Couldn't we go somewhere else?'

Dave looked at him briefly as if astounded at Ward's naivety.

'And face the big gangs up in the Midlands? The women have submachine guns poking out of their cunts up there.'

Ward wondered briefly if there were still factories producing all this lethal hardware; Liam's shotgun was geriatric but surely not all the weapons could be survivors from an earlier age. Shelving that thought he continued: 'And when we first met. Would you have really eaten me?'

Dave looked briefly at Liam who was a few steps behind. Both men grinned.

'Nah Dex. Things ain't that bad yet. But I've heard it goes on; in other gangs, like, not in ours.'

Not yet, Ward thought grimly, but it's coming.

Not for the first time, he wondered what crime he could have possibly committed to deserve this fate. The rainy streets of London were paradise compared to the furnace that was this doomed land. And what of the human race? Was that doomed as well? The climate would eventually stabilise and then slowly return to more moderate temperatures but how long would that take? A thousand years? Ten thousand?

They had been walking for an hour but had still not seen any wildlife. They stopped in a gently sloping hollow which, unusually, had a few pools of water at the bottom, choked with long strands of weed and with clouds of flies whirling above them.

They took sips of water from the flasks they carried at their waists. To Ward the water seemed as warm as that he used to bathe in, but it was all there was. Suddenly he received a violent blow on the shoulder. He spun around, fists balled, to find Liam holding a piece of wood with some pulpy reddish mess at one end.

'What the fuck!' Ward yelled.

Liam looked unconcerned. 'Where the hell do you come from, Ward?

45

Ain't you heard of mosquitoes, fella?' Then noticing Ward's blank expression, he sighed theatrically and said: 'Malaria.'

Ward grinned sheepishly. 'Thanks mate. I owe you.' All the while thinking *Of course! In this new climate there's bound to be malaria wherever mosquitoes can breed.*

The stop proved fruitful as they were able to catch a few small vole-like creatures, which they stored in their pouches. And then it was time to move on.

After another hour of trudging Ward became aware that the number of ruined buildings they were passing was increasing markedly. He realised that this was the remains of a town.

'Why are we going in here?' he finally asked.

'Dogs,' Dave explained' 'They like hanging around these piles of stone. Don't ask me why.'

Ward noted that the use of dogs as hunting partners was foreign to these people; the quarry was too small and isolated to make it worth sharing the kills with other mouths.

They walked on through the shattered streets, glad of the shade that the ruined walls cast. Finally, Liam said: 'Ain't no point in going on; we'd have heard 'em by now if there were any.'

Just as he said that Ward saw in the distance a large building that seemed vaguely familiar. Substantial amounts of masonry still reared up against the backdrop of the sea.

He searched his memories, trying to fit what he saw into some geographical pigeonhole.

Then suddenly he had it. He imagined a tall spire, rising proudly up from one end of the skeletal structure.

Norwich Cathedral.

This was, or rather had been, Norwich!

Ward had only been to the city once, but he was quite sure that it had not been a coastal town.

So much lost! So much destroyed! Ward was seized by an overwhelming desire to fling his catch-bag to the ground and run off, somewhere, anywhere. Whether it was the down part of his cycle or not, he didn't care. This reality was enough to drive anyone to suicide. He had to get out of this horrific corpse of a society, a country, a world. Like everyone around

46

him, he was a condemned man, with the only difference being that they didn't know it. But he did!

They walked slowly out of the ruins; no-one had much energy for conversation and in any case, what was there to talk about? The landscape never changed; their situation never changed. There was always the constant gnawing of hunger, the constant blast of the sun's rays on their heads and backs. Ward sensed that trouble was building: a failed hunt always brought short tempers to snapping point and they had walked a long way and had only caught a few voles, which would not be enough to satisfy a child.

It finally happened when they were about an hour out from the ruined city: one of the lower grade men stumbled and fell onto Dave, sending him sprawling.

Instantly Dave leapt up and delivered a fearsome uppercut to the unfortunate man and he too sprawled on the dusty ground. Dave's blood was up and he drew a knife from his belt. Ward watched helplessly; only Dave and Liam were senior enough to carry knives, everyone else was restricted to throwing sticks.

'Come on you bastard!' Dave yelled, advancing on the fallen man who was trying to crawl away without being able to get up, his eyes fixed on the knife. The other man and Liam watched disinterestedly; exhaustion and hunger had robbed them of the ability to develop any kind of excitement. Whether the man on the ground lived or died was obviously of no great concern to them. Ward watched in horror; he hadn't quite realised how cheap life was in this blasted land, but it seemed he was about to find out. It was then his peripheral vision caught a small movement.

'Stop!' he yelled, in a voice which carried so much authority that Ward himself was surprised. The others turned and saw what Ward had seen – a large plump doe; so plump she was probably pregnant.

Ward drew his throwing stick. He knew that his status in the group depended on what was to happen in the next few seconds. If he missed, his hard-won status as an expert hunter would be lost and he would be banished to the bottom of the hierarchy; back to where he had started in the ruined farmhouse. Dave and Liam's friendship would evaporate like drinking water thrown onto a stone. He might even be next in line for the knife.

He drew his arm back ready for the killing throw. One chance and one alone. He thought of his predecessor and his undoubted skill. *Muscle memory – don't fail me now*!

And with that he threw the stick.

It caught the doe neatly in the neck; it jerked once and fell dead on the parched ground.

The other men roared in approval and clustered around Ward, who felt like he had just scored the winning goal in the FA Cup. They clapped him on the back and gave lightweight punches on his arms. This plus the voles would mean they had not trekked out into the wilderness in vain. They would return as heroes!

The rest of the trip back was almost light-hearted, with genuine conversations taking place. As the camp came into view Ward felt a light touch on his arm and turning, found the man who had collided with Dave next to him.

'Thanks mate,' the rescued man said, 'You saved my life by hitting that bloody rabbit.'

Ward felt magnanimous; his position in the camp was now secure; even a few missed throws wouldn't be so bad now. He clapped the man on his shoulder and said: 'Forget it!' and was smugly satisfied to see the pitiful gratitude in the other's eyes. As he watched him hurriedly rush off to his dwelling Ward thought: *Yes, I've given you a few more days. A few more days to spend in this living Hell! And you thanked me.*

As the author of their success, that evening Ward was allowed to choose his piece of the doe, which had indeed been pregnant. A few small berries similar to those of the elder were added to his meal as a special reward.

But an even greater reward was to come.

As he lay in the shack he shared with some other men the tarpaulin was suddenly drawn back and Liam's head appeared.

'Out!' he snapped at the other men, 'Now!'

The others, all low graders, obeyed immediately. Then Liam drew the tarpaulin farther back and brought somebody in behind him.

'You did good work there Dex. You stopped Dave from doing something a little bit naughty. When I told the Professor, he said you deserved something more tasty than an extra bit of rabbit. And here she is.'

He stood aside to reveal a youngish woman, dressed in the usual rags; only her crotch was fully covered.

Liam gave her a little push towards Ward.

Here you are girl; this is the man. Make sure you're nice to him.'

And with that he left. Ward looked the woman up and down; he was not averse to this reward. She in turn looked him full in the eye; unabashed; unafraid. He drew her towards him, lifting the tangled birds-nest of brown hair so he could better see her face. It was a pleasant, symmetrical face under the grime with features that looked like they could have been made for laughter – if this had been a world one could find laughter in. As their bodies touched, he could tell that she stank, but then so did he. So did everyone. He pulled the cloth away from her breasts and then rolled on top of her as he pushed her down onto the straw. She continued to stare straight into his eyes.

Afterwards, Ward felt a flow of tenderness towards the woman, now that his need had been satisfied. Propping himself up on one elbow he watched her as she carefully rearranged the bits of cloth to cover herself.

'What's your name?' he asked, trying to sound warm and friendly.

'Eva, sir,' she replied as she made the final adjustment.

Eva? he thought, *sounds like 'Aoife'*. Was this another coincidence or another sign that some kind of weird plan was being executed with him as the mindless pawn?

He thought briefly of the beautiful, deadly wife that another Ward had once had, in another world, another reality. Where was she now? Did she and Gunter get away with murder and live out a life of endless luxury and passion on some Mediterranean hideout, far away from dying grass in a dying land?

Then he stopped wondering. All the hairs on his head and body had suddenly risen as if caught in a powerful electrical field. Through a gap in the tarpaulin curtain he could see the sky and instantly went through it to check if he had really seen what he had thought he had seen.

He had. There was a band of vivid green stretching over the zenith of the night sky. As Ward watched another band rose from the horizon to meet the first. As they met there was a sudden bright flash and they were gone. And Ward's hairs returned to normal.

49

Another strange thing, Ward thought, *and does this mean more trouble for me?*

Chapter Seven

Ward spent more and more time with Eva - which was against the rules of the tribe. Ward was not high enough to have his own woman. He knew that and he knew that trouble would ensue, but he didn't care. He was tired of male company and its brutal ways; its careless attitude to death; the constant jockeying for a higher rank in the social order. Only Eva and the Professor gave him someone he could talk to. But he had learned about all he could from the latter; he had learned over and over how the disaster which was slowly exterminating mankind could have been avoided – but had not been. He felt like someone dangling over a chasm attached to a rope that was slowly fraying; he knew that the fall was coming, that it was inescapable, both for him as an individual and for his species.

Eva knew nothing of the causes of the world she inhabited, why it was so miserable and wretched. Perhaps it was just as well she did not believe Ward's stories; for, casting caution to the furnace winds of Norfolk, he had begun to tell her of the world he had come from. He could not explain how he had got to Eva's world for he did not know himself, so he told her he came from a far-off land where the air was cool and the vegetation verdant and sometimes bedewed with soft rain.

'Will you take me there Dexter?' she had plaintively enquired one day, her hand entwined with Ward's. 'It sounds so beautiful; a place where it is so cold you cannot sleep out on the bare ground but must cover yourself! And the tall trees with all the lovely green leaves! How could you leave such a place!'

How indeed? Ward thought bitterly, I damn well didn't want to leave it. And what nightmare will I be flung into next?

Nothing had come of the strange lights in the sky that he had seen a while ago; it must have been an aurora. Ward had never seen an aurora, but he had been told they were often green. There had been another report of one of the Weird Ones shortly after but that too had come to nothing.

So Ward contented himself with Eva. They walked together; not far from the camp because there was nowhere to go; nothing to see. Ward ached to tell her more about himself, to have someone he could confide in and share this crushing load that he was staggering under. But he could only take her so far; there could be no mention of apparently dying and coming back to life – he did not want to lose her.

One day Liam had taken him aside and said 'Ward mate; you're getting too attached to that wee girl. She's common property see, and the other men are getting restless.'

Ward had nodded and vowed to continue exactly as he was. The fact that Eva had had sex with every able-bodied man in the camp didn't worry him; he had seen first affection dawn in her eyes when he was in her and then slowly something deeper. In their quiet times she had implored him to tell her more about the far-off country he came from. She listened wide-eyed when he told her how cats and dogs were not food where he came from but companions; one to take out on walks on cold March mornings; one to purr on one's lap at the end of the day. But she drew the line at snow and ice; those she would steadfastly not believe in.

'Dexter!' she would say, giving him a playful punch, 'Stop it! Be serious! How can you expect me to listen to you when you tell these silly stories?'

He would grin and kiss her and vow not to bring up the topic again. But he would: in the aftermath of their lovemaking he would look down on her and ache to tell her of the world he had lost. He would speak of the trees bursting into bud; of delicate shoots pushing up through the soil; of the glory of the countryside in summer when the heat was warm and comforting not a blazing knife pushed down one's windpipe. Then he would describe how the leaves would turn crimson and amber as autumn progressed and the birds would form lines on the telephone wires as they prepared to escape the gathering frost.

She would look at him, not entirely sure if he was playing with her, and ask things like 'What are telephones?' and he would hold her close, her hair spilling over his shoulder, and inside he would feel like weeping for the fate of stupid mankind; intelligent enough to cause existential problems but not intelligent enough to escape them. His people here had been doomed by the blind actions of their forefathers; and were now maimed and mutilated beyond all hope of redemption.

Dave and Liam were concerned about things far removed from gathering frosts. There were reports that a rival gang was moving into the area; big men with machetes and axes. Men who meant business and brooked no rivals.

They and Ward discussed tactics with the Professor.

'Have you seen them yet?' he enquired.

'One guy has,' Dave replied, 'Black guys with big knives.'

'But no guns?'

'No-one has seen any.'

'Then this is what we do.' The Professor leaned forward eagerly. 'We let them come in and surround them. Then open fire.'

Dave looked at Liam with a slightly worried expression and then back at the Professor. 'Yes, but we're low on ammunition, Prof. The guys we get the ammo from have left the area. They're afraid of the black guys. And we need the ammo for taking down the dogs.'

The Professor leaned back and placed a hand on his forehead. He evidently had still not got used to dealing with men less intelligent than he was. Then he leaned forward again.

'You let those men into this territory, and you'll be meat for the dogs! Do as I say, or you'll end up as a pile of dog turds!'

Liam and Dave gave quick nods and the discussion moved on to discussing the details.

***

The day dawned for the confrontation. Ward had been given the high honour of carrying one of the rifles. Ammunition was far too precious for target practice, so they were forced to accept his word that he was used to firearms. Apparently abundant ammunition was another one of the unusual things about Ward's homeland.

He was standing outside his hut, turning the rifle over so he could inspect all parts of it, when a heavy hand descended from behind him onto his shoulder. Turning around he found himself staring up at a bearded face that was contorted with anger. Ward was not surprised: anger and lust appeared to be the only emotions that anyone showed in this new society.

'Leave her alone, see,' the big man hissed. 'Eva. Leave her alone.'

Ward was unimpressed. He had faced so many perils that his threshold of fear had risen considerably.

'Or what?'

A fist was waved back and forth some millimetres from Ward's face.

'Or this will be just the start of what you'll get.'

'Are you part of our surprise party?' Ward asked, unabashed.

The man looked flustered.

'No.'

Ward grabbed the man's filthy tunic and attempted, unsuccessfully, to pull his face closer.

'Then go back to the women and leave the hard work to us men!'

The man snarled and turned away but when he was some distance away, he looked back and shouted: 'I'm not done with you Ward! Remember I warned you!'

Ward gave a rude gesture as the man disappeared and, forgetting him, went back to inspecting his rifle. Finally, he made sure that his knife was secure in his belt and then he knew that it was time to move out.

The armed party left the village, having been drilled in the Professor's plan by Dave and Liam. Scouts had already reported that the rival gang had been seen a few kilometres away and were heading straight for the village.

The Professor had told them they must wait for the gang to pass through an area of low-lying ground that stretched between two parallel ridges. They were to split in two as they approached this area and man the ridges as the rivals passed below.

And then kill them.

Ward strode beside Liam. His body had toughened up considerably since joining the tribe, but his knees still hurt when under exertion. He had not mentioned the affliction to anyone and never would. Weaknesses were to be got over and not admitted. Pity was in short supply in this hothouse world.

'No point in trying to talk to them, I guess,' he said to Liam. Liam looked quickly at him with an expression which showed a mixture of bemusement and contempt.

'Talk to them? While they're cutting your bollocks off, you mean!'

Karl suddenly appeared in front of them; he had been sent out ahead,

54

making use of his great speed to reconnoitre.

'They're just coming into the hollow now!' he said, as soon as he was close enough not to need to shout.

'Shit!' Liam hissed, 'they've moved fast!' He turned around and gestured to the bulk of the men that it was time to split into two sections. His waving motions indicated that they had to speed up. The two wings fanned out, trying to get up onto the ridges before the intruders exited.

Dave came up. 'We're not going to make it. They'll be out before we're ready.'

Liam cursed and looked desperately around. 'We've got to hold them there.' He stared at Ward. 'Are you game to stop them?'

Ward nodded. He thought of Eva's fate once the tribe's men had been slaughtered and the invaders had the camp to themselves.

'Come on!' Liam was off, heading straight for the mouth of the hollow and Ward followed behind, trying desperately to keep up. The two ridges rose slowly before them but already Ward could hear the excited shouting of the oncoming band, as they psyched themselves up for action.

And suddenly there they were. The vanguard had already reached the exit of the little valley and stopped in amazement at the sight of two men running straight at them.

But only for a second. Then they started hollering and yelling and clashing wicked looking axes and machetes together. The leader, a massive man seemingly carved from obsidian, stepped forward.

'Hey white boys! You hurry to die, yes?'

Liam and Ward had stopped within easy shouting distance of the rival gang.

'No, this your day to die!' Liam yelled.

The big man turned slightly to grin at his followers and then turned back, still grinning and showing a set of yellow teeth, sharpened to points.

'First we kill you. Then we eat you.'

He broke into a charge. Liam put his rifle to his shoulder and attempted to fire. Nothing happened. The man charged on, crossing the intervening distance with amazing rapidity.

In all happened in a blur. Ward followed him with the sights of his rifle and squeezed the trigger. This time there was no misfire. The big man fell like an axed sequoia.

The others gave a thunderous roar of anger and then surged forward.

Where are our men? Ward thought desperately. He fired again and again and more fell. And then they were on him. Almost immediately a sweeping blow from a machete knocked the rifle out of his hands and its wielder swung again to finish the job. Ward got inside the killing arc and drove his knee into the man's groin. Both were suddenly on the ground, hacking at each other's eyes.

And then there was the sharp crack of many rifles filling the air and cutting through the frenzied shouts. Our men have made it! Ward thought triumphantly and given new strength by this development he managed to reach the man's eyes and jabbed viciously into them. The knife finished the job.

He stood up. There was a faint bluish smoke in the air from the fusillade that had cut into the oncoming gang, many of whom were stretched out on the tawny grass, now developing red patches which were gradually spreading and sinking into the thirsty dust.

It was not the end; the tribe had to sweep down the sides of the ridges and engage in some hand to hand combat before the invaders were finally driven off.

And though the invaders had suffered the most, the tribe had, inevitably, borne wounds as well. Several were dead and Liam had lost all but one of the fingers on his right hand. His hunting days were over.

But Ward kept telling himself: the camp was safe!

Eva was safe!

When they got back the victorious men wanted to throw an orgiastic celebration, using up their stock of thin, berry wine but the Professor would not allow it. Only when the patrols came back and reported no sign of the enemy did he relax and allow them to go wild.

Liam did not go wild; he sat in his hut, looking at his bandaged hand and thinking about his future.

Ward did not go wild either; he thought it was not the right time for more lovemaking with Eva. He wanted it to be something for the two of them to gently explore together, both giving and receiving pleasure.

And so, soon after she had examined his taut body, they fell asleep, side by side.

Thus it was that they did not feel the hairs on their bodies rise up as if under a strong electric field.

Neither did they see bands of green illuminating the night sky, before vanishing with a sudden flash.

Chapter Eight

Ward faced the new day with a new sense of confidence and belonging. In part, like all men, he was riding a testosterone surge after defeating other males in a face to face struggle. Maybe it was also the high point of his cycle but as he looked around, he saw the passing tribe members as *his* people; he was one of them and he and they were united against all comers.

He mused for a while on his lot: it was not that bad – the killing heat was of course coming but it was not likely to arrive tomorrow or the day after. Plenty of time to live out a natural lifespan, and when frailty finally overtook him, well, someone had to replace the Professor and who better equipped than he?

And there was Eva of course. Something had happened there; there was a connection beyond the mere physical; a feeling that he never wanted to be apart from her; that he must protect her in this vicious arena from all the dangers and evils that pressed in so close.

The poor girl was still expecting him to pass her on to the next man. Every morning for quite some time she had faced him and said; 'Is this the day, Dexter? Must I leave you now?'

And he had taken her and pressed her small form against his chest and nuzzled her hair.

'No Eva,' he had said, 'this is not the day. And that day will never come. You will stay with me and we will be happy.'

And as she looked up at him, he had thought I pity the man who comes between you and me Eva for I will hunt him down and tear him to pieces. This I swear.

Several men had come up to him and asked if they could have Eva now and his fierce glare had driven them all off.

But perhaps not all. One man did not come to Ward and ask for Eva but watched the two of them as they walked together in the morning or rested in shadows away from the merciless flame of noon. And he waited.

When Ward sat with the Professor the latter could feel authority slipping from him to the younger man. It was Ward who was now coming up with the plans and stratagems and was even beginning to point out flaws in the Professor's own ideas. In token of this new relationship the Professor had offered to share the sacred tobacco with Ward and been surprised by Ward's polite refusal.

Ward knew that the tribe's defences were inadequate: as the Tropics became increasingly uninhabitable the mad flow of refugees could only increase to a great tsunami of desperate, starving wretches with nothing to lose. They would overwhelm the pitiful resources of his people and kill the men and enslave the women. Such had been the fate of the conquered throughout history.

It would not happen to his people!

Ward convinced the Professor that the only hope was to uproot the tribe and strike north; first into the lands of the fierce Midland tribes. There they would make allies, create alliances, form confederations but all the time moving north – north at all costs!

Ward knew the geography of Britain far better than the Professor and often when describing his ideas, he would smile a bitter smile as he thought of all the times he had driven through those areas, then so ordinary, so quotidian. Of the service stations he had stopped at for coffee and overpriced snacks; places that were now far off lands of strange dangers.

The Professor had nodded at the end of Ward's latest speech, noting the passion that underlay his words. He gave a small smile of approval.

'It was a fortuitous day when you came into our territory, Ward. I know that I cannot guide the people for much longer and before you came that gave me great sorrow. But I can go now with hope. You will save the people when I am gone. They deserve a leader like you.'

Ward had started to protest that the Professor had many more years in front of him, but the Professor held up a thin hand to stop him. 'No Ward. Don't say anything. What I admire in you is your ability to look the truth in the eye without flinching. Don't spoil it now.'

Ward had left with a feeling of mixed sadness and exhilaration: he knew he was the man the tribe needed but at the same time the thought that his conversations with the Professor were ending gave him a bittersweet sensation.

***

The others in the tribe seemed by some unknown osmosis to know that leadership was passing. They made no demur when he gathered them together to plan the day's activities. He had explained that it was possible to pen rabbits together rather than go out every day looking for them and in order to conserve ammunition they should develop bows and arrows.

He dismissed them and began to walk back to the hut, which was now his and Eva's alone.

It was then a tremendous blow struck his head and he collapsed onto the ground in a cloud of dust. He lay there face down, his nostrils full of the choking dust while daggers seemed to plunge in and out of his brain. He felt himself being dragged to his feet like a rag doll and being held by one hand as another drew back and smashed full in his face. Blood sprayed out in a fine mist as his head was knocked back and he crashed heavily back onto the ground.

This time he managed to roll onto his back and look up at his assailant.

It was the big man who had wanted Eva.

'I warned you Ward!' the man roared in thunderous tones, 'You wouldn't listen! Nobody comes between me and a woman! Who the fuck are you anyway! You come in here begging for food and now you think you're running the place. Well, you're dead wrong – and now you'll be just dead!'

With that he pulled out a long, shining knife. By its condition it hadn't seen much work – but it appeared that it was just about to.

Ward was too dazed to fight back. This it seemed was where his strange story was going to end. How unexpected.

Then something leapt onto the big man's back, a screaming thing of thrashing fury, with a hand that held another knife; one that struck and struck and struck again at the man's throat until the blood was a veritable fountain.

It was Eva.

The man fell slowly, vainly clutching his ruined throat. He ended in a kneeling position as his knife fell from bloodied fingers. Eva stood before him, arms akimbo.

60

He heard her yell triumphantly: 'You attacked my man. For that you die!'

Ward heard no more; he lay back on the hot dust and darkness took him.

***

When he awoke, he more than half expected to have undergone another transition.

But no – he was still with the tribe; still trapped in an oven with laughing demons busily turning up the thermostat.

He was in his own hut lying on the bed of dry grass. Dave was bending over him.

'Still with us then, you lucky fucker!'

Ward got up slowly and carefully.

'I'm alright then?'

'You've got a few less teeth, I think. But apart from that just bruising. What do you expect? His knife got nowhere near you.'

Ward felt his jaw. By the feel of it, it seemed Dave was right. Oh well. Then he remembered.

'How's Eva?'

Dave's grin vanished. 'She's OK. For the time being.'

Ward grabbed Dave by the shoulder.

'What does that mean?'

Dave carefully removed Ward's hand from his shoulder.

'What do you expect? She killed a man. That means she gets it too.'

'What! Execution!'

'Of course. We can't have women killing men. It's unnatural. She's got to pay the price.'

'When?'

'Tomorrow at sunrise. The usual time. She …'

But Ward was already gone, heading for the Professor's hut.

That gentleman was having a nap when Ward burst in like a madman.

'Ward, it's not time for our talk.'

'To hell with talking! I want Eva – where is she!'

The Professor shook off the cobwebs of sleep and looked calmly at the intruder.

'In the pen – like all criminals.'

'Criminal? She saved my life, you stupid old bastard!'

The professor smiled indulgently. 'Ward you are a good man and I have great hopes for you, but you are still a newcomer and you don't understand all our ways. No woman may kill a man, for any reason whatsoever. She did indeed save your life and I and the whole tribe are grateful for that. We cannot lose you. But you understand that even though I like you I cannot be seen to have favourites. I cannot change the law for one man. She dies tomorrow morning. I would do the same to my own woman, if I had one.'

Ward stared at the old man. Fire seemed to be raging through his veins; one more stupid word from the Professor and he would kill him where he lay.

'She will not die. Do you hear me – she will not die! I will tear this camp apart and kill every man in it if I have to! She will not die!'

And with that he was gone.

As Ward marched out into the sweltering night a firm calculation swept away the magma of his anger.

They must head north as soon as he had got her out of her captivity. They must keep going until they found another tribe which they could join. Other men would take an interest in Eva, but he was prepared for that: they would learn the hard way that this woman was not for sharing.

To begin with they would move by day as well as night until they had put enough distance between them and this encampment. Only then would they be able to seek shelter from the engulfing heat. But they would need food and water before they could find another tribe.

Ward went back to his hut and rammed as much dried meat into his catch bag as it would take. He checked that the water flask contained enough of the precious liquid. Fortunately, it did so he did not need to waste valuable time raiding the communal tank. He slung his rifle over his shoulder and pushed his knife into its holster: he would use the rifle; Eva would wield the knife.

He took a quick look around the hut: it had been his home for only a few months, but he knew that whatever happened he would never see it again. Then he set off for the pen.

He gave curt acknowledgements to the people he passed on the way but luckily there were few about. The pen was situated near the centre of the camp so everyone could get a clear view of the ceremony tomorrow. In its centre was a pole and tied to it with leather straps – Eva!

Then he cursed under his breath – there was a guard! He had felt certain that there would not be one as the mores of female execution was accepted by the whole tribe so the idea that someone would attempt a rescue was unthinkable.

But there was a guard.

He retreated into the shadows while he considered his options. He didn't want to kill the man, who no doubt had fought well in the Battle of the Pass, but neither could he allow him to raise the alarm. Ward had seen many movies in which tough guys had knocked another man unconscious with a single blow, but he doubted that he was capable of such a feat.

He looked around for a non-lethal weapon and found one in the form of a sturdy branch which had been left lying on the ground after the repairs to a nearby hut had been completed. Now all that was needed was to slowly approach the guard from behind…

The man heard Ward's approach and began to turn but it was too late. The branch snapped in half as it smashed down onto his head and, soundlessly, he toppled to the dust. Ward looked down at him briefly: it had been a hell of a blow; maybe he had killed him after all. No time to worry – he vaulted over the low wicker fence and was at Eva's side in an instant. She was asleep and he placed a hand over her mouth before waking her. Her eyes opened wide in astonishment at the fact that someone was breaking the taboos of the tribe and rescuing her and under his hand Ward felt her lips spell out the word 'Dexter!'

The knife gleamed in the yellow moonlight and she was free. Ward pointed in the vague direction of north and she nodded. Shadows among the shadows, they crept out of the pen for unknown lands and dangers unknown – but the latter was more than he could ever have imagined.

Chapter Nine

They tried to keep up a steady pace in the suffocating, crippling heat but it was impossible. In the end they settled for moving from one slightly shaded area to the next slightly shaded area; sometimes the shade came from a group of stunted trees; sometimes from a large rock rearing out of the parched veldt. On reaching whatever was casting its welcome shadow they would lie in the blessed dimness, feeling the sweat on their bodies dry into curling white flakes; perhaps they would even sleep for a short while.

The water was rationed of course, as there was little chance of replenishing the supply until they reached the next tribe. Once Eva managed to catch a vole which they ripped apart and ravenously ate the edible parts, plus a little bit of the inedible parts as well.

They saw a few people in the distance but no organised pursuit party. Eventually they decided that their erstwhile companions had decided that they did not have enough resources to effect a pursuit. Ward even felt a little pang of regret that he had left behind people who had seen him as their next leader. Without flattering himself he could not think of anyone who could easily replace him; poor Liam with his maimed hand would find himself rapidly consigned to the lower orders.

Once as Eva lay sleeping with her tousled hair spreading over his lap Ward thought he heard a strange humming noise, as if powerful electrical machinery were nearby. But that was impossible – this impoverished, retrograde land had no such machines or the intelligence to plan them or the skills to build them. They lay there for quite some time until the sun set, and the sky empurpled. A dismal crescent moon, yellowed by the dust in the air, shone wanly down on the stricken land, looking like an old broken-off fang. Ward looked at it, finding it impossible to believe than men had once walked on its surface, supposedly heralding in a new age, but in fact achieving nothing. He wondered briefly if the men of this world had visited it before catastrophe had struck them down.

The next morning found him even more exhausted and dispirited than he had been the previous evening. As they slowly walked along Ward stole the occasional glance at Eva. She looked indomitable, apparently willing to follow him into the mouth of Hell itself. Ward wondered on several occasions whether he was in fact worthy of this devotion; after all she had saved his life at great personal risk, not vice versa. But once, when she caught him looking at her, she had smiled and all was well. Ward knew then he loved Eva; perhaps for the first time in his life he understood what love meant. He thought of his wives – Siobhan, the original before all this insanity had begun, and the beautiful, deadly Aoife. He had not known Aoife all that long but even before he had realised that she wanted to kill him he had known that with her it was only sex.

They walked slowly and tiredly on; not daring to wonder how far they had travelled.

And then it happened.

They crested a low ridge and looked down into a small hollow.

In the hollow was something totally unexpected – a metal cube, perhaps four metres in its dimensions. As they walked towards it, its colour shifted from golden-amber to a coppery red. They walked right up to it and stopped a few metres away, wonderingly.

'It's lovely,' said Eva admiringly, 'What is it Dexter?'

Dexter did not reply. He hated not to seem all-knowing in front of Eva, but he had no more idea than she.

As he got closer, he began to be aware that a faint humming was emanating from this mysterious artefact and the hairs on his arms began to elevate. At first, he thought it was just the strangeness of the situation but glancing at Eva he could see that the tangled mass of her chestnut locks was beginning to straighten and rise.

It was then he stopped.

A terrible fear rose up in him, like a risen parasite clutching his throat from within. *This was wrong! Wrong! Nothing like this should exist in this sun-blasted world.*

He turned abruptly. 'Eva! We must get away! There's danger here!'

She smiled gently up at him. She could see no danger in this shining mass of lustrous metal. He could see little reflections of the strange cube in her eyes.

'Danger, Dexter? How can that be? What sort of danger?'

He grabbed her arm and pulled her away from the cube.

'Don't argue! We must go – now!'

Although she looked a little shocked by his rough handling, she nodded. She trusted Ward to look out for her. He decided to skirt the object and carry on in approximately the same direction as they had been travelling.

Slightly pulling Eva behind him as she turned her head to look at the cube one last time, he strode toward the other lip of the hollow.

And stopped.

Three figures had appeared on the lip looking down on them.

Three preternaturally tall figures with long arms and helmets which covered their faces except for a visor for their eyes.

'Dexter who are they?' Eva whispered, 'Dexter – I'm frightened!'

But in the shock Ward's knees had given way and he was crouched beside her, staring at the ground.

The Weird Ones! The Weird Ones! They've followed me! His head felt like it was on the verge of exploding as that thought echoed and re-echoed through his mind.

'Dexter!' Eva's voice brought him back from the brink – he must protect Eva.

He stood up and watched the three figures approach.

The nearest lifted a small metallic object which it held, and there was a sharp noise like the cracking of a whip. Eva gave a muffled cry and Dexter turned in time to see a crimson flower of blood blossom on her chest.

She was dead before she hit the ground.

He stood for a moment overwhelmed by the unreality of it all.

Eva dead.

The Weird Ones.

Then the blind, red rage took him and shook his whole body like a rat in a terrier's jaws.

Eva was dead.

He would kill these creatures, rip off their filthy heads, tear out their guts and shit into their body cavities!

He did none of those things.

As he ran towards them the second in line lifted another small metallic object.

There was a different sound and Ward crashed to the ground unconscious.

***

Ward rose unwillingly to the surface of the lake of unconsciousness into which he had been thrown. There was some terrible truth awaiting him if he burst through the surface into full awareness.

He did not want that and tried to swim back down into the depths.

He could not.

His eyes opened.

He was strapped to a couch in a large room, in which everything – the floor, the walls, the ceiling, and the body of his couch was made of metal. He could move his head from side to side, but he could see nothing but more couches and banks of softly glowing machinery. There were no windows.

I've transitioned again! he thought, inwardly groaning.

But no! As he glanced down, he could see the thin white lines of the familiar scars on his chest. This was the same body as he had had in Norfolk – he had not transitioned.

But if so where in God's name was this place?

Then he remembered Eva and he tried to rise from the couch in blind fury.

The straps stretched but did not break and he crashed back down, finally sobbing as the horror of it all seized him with talons of eviscerating pain.

He resigned himself to staring at the featureless metal ceiling.

Hours passed. Unable to move, he urinated over himself.

More time passed.

And then suddenly an upside-down head appeared in his field of vision, staring down at him. He realised that for the first time he was seeing one of the Weird Ones without any facial covering. And he wished he wasn't. The head moved to a more upright position as its owner moved to Ward's side.

The head that looked down on him bore a face that was vaguely

67

reptilian. There were no obvious scales, but the brown skin had a sharkskin-look about it as if greater magnification would indeed reveal very small scales. The eyes were narrow with vertical pupils and seemed to have a membrane that suddenly and rapidly flicked over them from time to time. The mouth was almost lipless and occasionally revealed sharp teeth, all the same size and shape. There were external ear pinnae, but they were almost flat against the roughly ovoid skull.

And that face was far too close to Ward's own.

The thin lips parted, sending waves of an odour resembling rotting fish over him.

The voice was high pitched and very soft and quiet, like a light wind heard through the canopy of an overarching tree.

'You are awake at last.'

Ward stared in a frozen horror at that face. Was it some kind of Halloween mask that would be removed to reveal the face of a laughing prankster? Surely it could not be real!

The ghastly face continued to stare at Ward, waiting for some kind of response.

Ward could see small muscle movements under the sharkskin tissue.

The face was real.

His captivity was real.

The horror was real.

'What do you want?' he finally managed to utter, in a voice so weak and tremulous that he hardly recognised it as his own.

The face withdrew a little, revealing more of a thin torso which was covered in a kind of metallic-looking tunic. The being was at least two metres tall but very slender and delicately built.

'We want you Ward,' came the whispery voice again, 'or rather we want your mind. To be more precise we want your brain.'

Ward absorbed that unusual information stolidly. It might mean many things; not necessarily the literal meaning.

'Where am I' he asked wearily, 'Where is this place?'

'To give you the most important information first, this is the second planet from the sun.'

Ward frowned. Venus? He was interested in popular astronomy and knew Venus was a world of terrible heat; heat so great that the rocks were on the verge of being red hot.

'How can this be Venus?' he eventually asked.

'We know of the planet to which you are referring. This is not that planet.'

'Then which planet is it?'

'It is Earth – but not your Earth.'

'And who are you.'

'We are The People.'

Ward gave up; he was not in any state to enjoy word games.

'Look, can you let me up? I've been on this couch for hours. And I'm starving.'

'Of course. It was always our intention to free you from this confinement. '

And with that, four-fingered hands undid the straps and helped the man to his feet. As Ward leaned against his strange captor, he was conscious of a definite body heat; whatever this thing was it was not a reptile. Shakily he straightened himself and looked up at that inhuman face.

'What do you want of me?' he couldn't help blurting out.

He had to know!

The creature looked steadily down at him, with those cat-like eyes seemingly reading his every thought.

'Our purpose will be made clear soon enough. Now you must eat and drink. Follow me.'

And with that it turned its back on him. Ward wondered for a second whether he should jump his jailer but decided against it: there were bound to be more of them, and he still had no idea where he was.

As he followed the being down a high-ceilinged metal corridor, he became aware of two things: One – the temperature was at least as high as that of the Norfolk he had just quitted and Two – he felt lighter somehow, as if there were springs on his feet. Despite the latter, he knew he was very close to complete exhaustion; since the flight from the camp he had not had enough of either food or water – he had made sure Eva had received more than her share.

Eva! The very thought of her name brought him near to tears; both for her loss and for his unending series of trials – each one apparently fated

69

to be grimmer than that preceding.

The corridor opened out into a wider room; also without windows, just as his prison cell had been.

There were benches in the centre and around the sides were devices with nozzles and shelves with bowls and cups on them.

The creature picked up a bowl and said 'Watch.' Holding the bowl under the larger of the two nozzles it pressed a button on the side of the device and the bowl was immediately filled with a brown, steaming paste. It then picked up a cup and did the same thing with the smaller of the two nozzles. It passed both receptacles to Ward.

'The solid is a highly nutritious yeast paste; the liquid is de-ionised water.'

Ward sipped the water; it was stale and warm; but it was water. Picking up a spoon from a nearby tray he began to devour the yeast paste; it had a similar flavour to the brewers' yeast supplements that he had taken once, and he quickly cleaned the bowl.

'You may sit down now,' his jailer commented, 'but you can fill your bowl as often as you desire. The room directly behind is a lavatory for the use of your species and others with similar needs. We will not disturb you there.'

Thanks a bunch, Ward thought bitterly, Am I supposed to be grateful? Will you be supplying me with an exercise wheel next?

'We will leave you to rest now,' the creature continued, obviously unaware of Ward's ingratitude, 'we shall call on you soon. In the meantime, you may have some company.'

With that it strode off in the direction of a metal door, which opened just before it reached it, and disappeared down yet another metallic corridor.

After filling his bowl again Ward sat down on one of the benches wondering, not for the first time, what was in store for him.

He heard another door shush open and did not look up.

Then he heard a human, male voice: 'Holy Immortal - another man!'

Chapter Ten

Ward looked around in wonder to see a slim, clean-shaven man dressed in shorts and a T-Shirt rapidly approaching him.

He leapt up, suddenly conscious of the fact that his Norfolk clothing did not entirely cover his genitals.

The man came up to him and started pumping his right hand.

'What is name?' the newcomer asked eagerly, 'I not know another guy here!'

Dexter gave him his answer and then said, 'And yours?'

'Miloslav, Miloslav Averin.'

'Russian?'

'Da, and you - American?'

'English. And how did you get here?'

Averin gave a confused story in halting English of how he had several times thought he had been killed only to find that he was still alive. And of how he had become aware of strangely shaped men following him. And of how he had come upon a lustrous metal cube in the forest and...

'And then you found yourself here,' Ward finished for him.

'Da. And you, same?'

Ward gave him a condensed version of his history, which included Aoife but not Eva. That was too raw to mention to a stranger. 'And how long have you been here?'

Averin explained it was hard to tell as there was no day or night, but he reckoned about two months.

'And what have they done to you?' was Ward's next eager question.

'They put things like headphones on head and make me see things. Things that I don't want to see. Like war.'

'You've been in a war then?' Ward inquired; perhaps this guy's story was sadder than his.

'Da, Great Patriotic War against Germans and Japanese. It was terrible, Tsar Yerik just got out of Moscow hours before Fascists took it. Slaughter was terrible.'

Ward frowned inwardly. It had happened again; the "Not Quite Right History" problem. The Romanovs had been long gone by the time of the Nazi invasion of the Soviet Union, and Moscow had not fallen.

Despite there being more important things to discuss, he found himself asking: 'But you won the war.'

'Da, but only after atomic bombing of Berlin and Tokyo. Terrible, terrible times.'

Ward gave up; it was similar to the history that he had learned at school – but it wasn't similar enough to put it down to garbled remembrances. The Soviets had not developed the atomic bomb and they had not bombed either Berlin or Tokyo. He brought the conversation back to more pressing matters.

'So what do these bastards actually want?'

Averin finally sat down and spread large hands in bemusement.

'Not know. They say want to study mind. My mind special, they say. I don't know what special about it. No. Psychiatrist say my condition not unusual.'

'They have a psychiatrist here?'

'No not here. In Saint Petersburg. He say – what is words – Manic-Depressive common.'

Manic-Depressive! Ward thought, The old name for Bi-Polar! That simply could not be a coincidence!

'Me too, 'he finally said, 'Shake.'

And they did.

Averin finally took in Ward's odd attire.

'Very hot where you come from, yes?'

Ward nodded. 'But so is this place.'

Averin nodded. 'Very, very hot. I don't like it. Much colder in Saint Petersburg.'

For some reason they both found that comment amusing and Ward laughed out loud; for the first time that he had in many months, he ruefully realised.

72

'Are there any more like us?' he finally asked.

'There are others; I have seen them. But they are not like us.'

Ward frowned. 'In what way?'

'They are not – men. They have two arms, two legs – but they are not men.'

Ward no longer found that hard to believe; having seen his captors close up he was quite ready to believe in other captives who likewise were not entirely human.

'They don't have any contact with us,' Averin added helpfully, 'I've just seen them passing in the corridor. They don't eat our food.'

Averin got himself some of the yeast paste as did Ward and both ate silently.

They had run out of things to say; Averin was as trapped here as Ward was and had no solution to their joint dilemma.

After a while Ward forced himself to speak and enquired as delicately as he could about Averin's personal life. He had been a mathematician in the pay of the Russian government. He had been married but had lost his wife in the great siege of Volgograd which had only ended when the Nazis destroyed the entire city. He had met someone like her in one of his "other lives" but that too had ended sadly when she left him for a Volga German.

Ward spoke of his murderous wife, which caused Averin to pat him on the shoulder in brotherly affection, but he did not speak of Eva.

Their sporadic conversations were interrupted when a door suddenly opened. Two of the Weird Ones entered; at first, they looked absolutely identical as if they were all cloned from one template but then Ward noticed that one was slightly taller than the other; so they *were* individuals.

'Ward, we have to show you to your room now,' the taller one said.

Show me to my room? Ward thought acidly, Will there be a rose and a single dark chocolate on the bed?

Nevertheless, he followed the one who had spoken, while the other one drew Averin aside and seemed to be speaking very quietly to him.

Ward tagged behind his leader and as they passed down the corridor, he could see rectangular impressions in the walls, which must indicate the presence of rooms. They stopped and the being pressed a small button on the wall with a long, bony finger at which a door slid sideways revealing a room with a bed and a chair and a bidet-like object which Ward took to

73

be his lavatory. There were no windows.

'Your room,' the Weird One announced, somewhat unnecessarily. Ward went in warily.

There was no rose. No chocolate. But there was a neatly folded set of clothes on the chair which when unfolded was revealed to be shorts and a T-Shirt of an identical design to that which Averin had been wearing. The material looked like spun metal from a distance but when Ward fingered the fabric it had the feel of fine cotton.

'Change your clothes,' his guide ordered, 'We find your odour offensive.'

No doubt so would I – if I could smell myself, Ward thought. He stripped naked, feeling strangely embarrassed in front of his impassive companion and was about to pull the T-Shirt on when the other abruptly said 'No!' and pointed to a cubicle which Ward had failed to notice before. 'Wash first. The shower water contains an insecticide as we can see you are infested.'

'And after I do that and change, what then?' Ward demanded, 'Is there any entertainment laid on? Do you have the latest movies?'

'No entertainment. You are here to be studied.'

'And why me? Why have you followed me?'

'Your mentalic field is very strong; in fact, the strongest we have discovered. We are surprised to find it extends about twenty centimetres from your frontal lobes. That why is was so easy to track you through the probabilities.'

Another totally meaningless answer, Ward thought with increasing bitterness and anger, why do all these people speak in this gobbledy-gook? If they're suggesting I'm some kind of superman, I seem to be a very helpless one.

He shrugged and moved back to practicalities.

'And when does this studying begin?'

'In the morning. You will have enough time to sleep. We will come for you.'

'Oh joy.' Ward snapped, but the irony made no impression on the emotionless face of the other, who picked up the tattered remains of Ward's Norfolk clothes and made to leave.

'Wait!' shouted Ward, 'What will you do with those?'

74

The other turned back slightly. 'Incineration.'

Ward nodded dejectedly. Of course. What else could be done with such filthy rags? It was just that Eva had touched them. When they were destroyed so would be the last tangible link that he had with that woman.

The other left and the door closed silently behind him.

Ward sat down, naked and alone in a windowless room in an unknown location guarded by inhuman beings.

And he wept.

***

Ward had a shallow sleep, haunted by terrible dreams and sudden shuddering periods of wakefulness. During those periods he could see that the room was suffused with a soft violet glow which revealed the stark emptiness of his lodging.

Then, all too soon, the night – if that's what it was – was over.

The door opened and one of the Weird Ones came in, unannounced. Was it a different one? – Ward could not tell but it did not matter: this one had the same imperious attitude as the others.

He walked an indeterminate distance down the same type of featureless metal corridor as before; it seemed a very long walk but with his shredded nerves it was impossible to tell.

He was led into a large room with many couches and next to each one a machine with TV type screens and softly glowing lights that flashed off and on in different sequences and with lightning rapidity. He was made to lie down on the nearest and then, much to his concern, he was strapped down. Then sensors were attached to his scalp; to Ward's relief this did not require his head to be shaved.

And then it began.

There was a brilliant flash which seemed to emanate from within his skull and travel outwards, illuminating the entire room into a harsh monochrome.

Then there was darkness; a deep blackness unrelieved by even a single photon.

And then images began to form. Ward realised that he could both experience the images directly and study them from outside like a disinterested observer.

He was in a comfortable darkness when suddenly he felt a tremendous pressure all around, but chiefly behind, and he was being forced, much against his will, down a flexible tunnel that was both warm and wet. Suddenly there was blinding light and a terrible noise assailing his ears from all directions. He was held upside down and slapped while a finger forced its way into his mouth and dragged out some thick goo.

Ward the observer realised that he had just been born.

Other images flashed by, in a kaleidoscopic blur.

The images steadied, clarified, became focussed.

He was lying on his back and friendly, well-known faces were looking down on him and there was a hand squeezing his naked foot. Mouths were opening, closing, but he could not understand the words.

He was in his cot being adored by his parents.

And so it went on. He was shown himself being taken to nursery school, then trying to run back to his house and being adroitly captured by one of his teachers. He was shown himself noticing hair beginning to develop in his pubic region and he once again felt puzzlement as to why such a thing was happening.

Then he was back in the room and the faces looking down on him were not the kind, loving faces of his parents but the cold, inhuman visages of his captors.

For a few moments he was too disoriented to speak; his jaw and lips moved but there were only inchoate sounds. Then his whirling mind stabilised and he accepted the cold reality of his situation.

'Did you get all you wanted?' he finally managed to utter, turning his head so that those awful faces did not fill his field of vision.

'No of course not. That was merely a calibration test. We have much to learn about your mind and its properties. This will take some time.'

Ward wanted to scream Why are you doing this to me? I'm just an ordinary man! But he could not form the words in his semi-dazed state.

Thickly, he muttered 'How long will all this take?'

One of the beings was removing the sensors from his scalp while the other stood over him; the latter replied 'We do not know. We will be as quick as it is possible to be. We are in great danger and you are a key part of our plan to escape that danger.'

'What danger?'

'The Higgs,' replied the other and, obviously believing that the answer just given was sufficient, indicated to Ward that he could rise from the couch.

Higgs! Ward thought, Charles Dickens again! When will anything make bloody sense!

As he got unsteadily to his feet, he caught sight of himself in the shining surface of one of the machines; it was the first time in what seemed a very long time that he had seen his reflection. He had the tangled, straggly beard of a Norfolk tribesman; another proof, should any have been needed, that he had not transitioned.

'Is there anywhere I can shave in this place?' he demanded angrily, 'or will that disturb your fucking experiments!'

'You do not want the hair on your face?' one of the captors enquired.

'Yes goddammit!' Ward snapped, and then, realising the possibility of a misunderstanding, 'Just what's on my face – the stuff on top of my head I want to keep.'

'If that makes you more comfortable, it will be arranged. It is not difficult.'

Ward was accompanied back to his room and on entering, found a tumbler of water and a small bright-orange pill.

'As you requested,' his companion observed.

Ward glanced at the creature, but as always, there was no expression.

Was this another failure of communication, he wondered.

'Take it,' the Weird One commanded, 'We have other things to attend to. We will not offer again.'

Ward swallowed the pill which had a pleasant orangey taste and washed it down with the warm water.

'And now what?' he enquired.

'You will see.'

And with that he was alone.

After some time, spent mainly in staring at the wall of his room (or was it "cell"?) he felt a few pangs of hunger. The Weird Ones were apparently too busy to chaperone him anymore, but they had given him a device which by means of flashing indicators would allow him to find his way around the warren of identical-looking corridors.

After a few false turns, he did indeed find his way to the room where food was available; unfortunately, as he soon discovered, the only thing on the menu was the hot yeast paste which seemed to meet human dietary needs but was so unappetising that only hunger could drive a man to actually eat it.

Fortunately, Averin was already there and Ward's spirits lifted at the thought of some relief from the crushing boredom of his confinement.

'Dexter!' the other shouted as he saw Ward approach, 'good to see you again! How are you doing?'

Ward gave him a quick resume of the events of the last few hours.

'Is that what they've done to you?' he eventually enquired.

Averin nodded. 'Da. It is very strange to see things from past I had forgotten all about. Many things I not want to remember. Like Tamara leaving me for bloody German!'

Ward gave him a friendly pat on the shoulder. 'Yeah – that's a bummer.'

Averin clearly didn't understand colloquial English but after a few seconds he guessed Ward was sympathising with him and grinned.

'Da, bummer!'

Ward tried once again to understand more about the circumstances of his predicament.

'What's all this stuff about us being on Venus?'

'Venus?'

'Yes – they said this was the second planet from the sun.'

Averin looked puzzled and then broadly grinned again. 'Ah – it's a long story. You got time?'

Ward looked around in mock scrutiny of his surroundings and then back at Averin. 'Yeah, I think I've just got enough time.'

Averin began 'This is not our - what you say – reality? Things different here. Have you heard of Theia?'

Ward shrugged. 'No. Who is she?'

Averin looked slightly pained. 'Not person. Theia was planet that collided with Earth in the beginning. Bits left over from crash made moon.'

Ward remembered the theory from his popular astronomy although he didn't see how anyone could know what the rogue planet was called.

'Yes – I have heard that. It formed the moon and brought a lot of water to Earth. The moon stabilises the axis and makes Earth better suited for life - or so I'm told.'

'Da. But that not happen here. In this reality Theia not hit Earth. It passed close many time and de- de-'

'Destabilised,' Ward broke in helpfully.

'Yes - destabilised - inner parts of Solar system. Venus got chucked out and Earth moved closer to sun. Theia became third planet from sun.'

'So that's what they meant when they said that this was Earth but not Earth,' Ward said, with an odd feeling of triumph now that he had solved a very small part of the puzzle, 'And because Earth didn't merge with Theia it remained a smaller planet – which explains the lesser gravity.' He looked sharply at Averin. 'Have you seen anything of this planet – what's it like?'

Averin shook his head slowly. 'There is viewpoint which they allow personnel to use as reward for good behaviour. I've been on it few times.'

'And what did you see?'

Averin sighed and leaned away from Ward. 'A small town. And then desert. Nothing but desert.'

Somehow that news depressed Ward even further.

A small town on a stillborn world.

And then desert.

Endless desert.

Chapter Eleven

The next day was similar to the previous except that it was worse. Ward spent much longer on the examination couch, seeing more and more of his life, in chronological order.

He saw the succession of jobs that he had had in a wearisome sequence. He saw himself arrive fresh-faced, hopeful and eager. He saw the doubts begin to be written on the faces of his line managers; he saw the interviews in the small rooms and finally the notices of dismissal.

To his horror he realised he was going to have to relive the evening of his supposed suicide. As a god-like observer he saw himself take out his handgun and spend a long time staring down at it. Finally, he/Ward appeared to have made the fateful decision and picked up the weapon and placed it against his right temple. But then he saw the gun fire, saw the scarlet spray and saw he/Ward fall, collapsed face-down on the table.

But that had not happened! How could he be seeing something that had not occurred?

The images moved on, returning to his own memories. He saw again the Admiral Benbow with Betty and Arthur once more refusing him credit. His heart ached as he saw the familiar grey streets, the comforting faces of a world that now seemed as unreal as a lovely dream that tugs the emotions on awakening, as the quotidian world floods back.

Once again, the scene changed. Before his astounded inner vision once more Aoife stood before him, vigorously towelling herself after showering. Eagerly he drank in the sight of her ample breasts, hanging down like soft, pink fruit. To his horror, he saw himself seizing her and forcing himself upon her struggling body. How could Eva have ever loved a man such as he?

Then it was over. The images were snatched away, and he was on the couch again; bound by restraining straps with the cold, hard faces of The People staring down.

After he was released, he sat on the edge of the couch, head in hands, shaking. The images of his past life in a world that he had thought he had understood, were profoundly moving. He wanted to go back so much; to walk the streets of London again; to walk into his local pub and sit in the corner with his drink, idly flicking the pages of his newspaper. Instead he was on some unknown world that should not exist, surrounded by things that held him prisoner like a laboratory rat in a cage, and, apparently, with as much care for him as experimenters would feel for their rat.

To get the image of his rape of Aoife out of his brain he asked a question he really didn't care about.

'What was that cube thing we saw just before I came here?'

'It was the vehicle we use to move physically between the probabilities.'

Here we go again, Ward thought wearily. 'So you press a button and - whizzo! You're somewhere else. You are so clever.'

'It is not that simple as we are sure you must realise. Physically moving between the probabilities is very energy intensive and it is only temporary. The length of time we can spend in any given probability is directly proportional to the energy we supply to the machine; it takes the combined output from many fusion reactors to spend a single day in a different probability before we are pulled back into our native state.'

Ward realised that there might be a part of this answer that actually interested him.

'I noticed electrical disturbances in computers and in the sky before seeing you. Was that your bloody machine?'

'Ordinarily our appearance in a new physical reality would be forbidden by the First Law of Thermodynamics as it would involve the creation of mass-energy. So as part of the process we transfer an equivalent amount of material to our native existence. Any random amount of interplanetary rubble will suffice. However, the amounts must balance to below the yoctogram level and that is impossible to attain. So there is always a spontaneous flow of electromagnetic energy between the realities to ensure the balancing is exact. That accounts for the phenomena you observed.'

Ward thought for a moment and he came to the conclusion that he now knew less than he had before he asked the question. He wouldn't ask for any more information that might result in having to listen to this sort of gibberish ever again.

He was allowed to go back to his room by himself again; he tried finding his way without the little guiding machine and almost succeeded.

Just a few more trips, he thought, and I'll know my way around.

He threw himself down on the bed and lay there for a while resting his head on his interlinked arms. Once again, a wave of self-pity rose in his mind and for a moment, he thought his eyes had gone moist. But he fought the feeling back down and controlled it.

No, no more, he told himself, I'm not going to get out of this alive. I must accept that. Perhaps if the universe really is this crazy there is some place where I'll meet Eva again.

Eventually he fell into a shallow sleep in which, fortunately, no images appeared to torment him.

When he awoke, he was startled to see something hairy on his chest and for a mad moment thought he was being attacked by vermin. As he jumped up the hairy thing dissolved into individual hairs and fell to the floor.

He rubbed his chin. The beard had gone and his chin was completely smooth.

'Well I'll be …' he said to the empty room.

***

When he walked in to the eating place for his latest meal of yeast paste Averin rose to meet him and laughed.

'I see you have shave treatment!' he said, rubbing his own chin.

'Yes- you too?' Ward replied, gloomily watching the paste slop into his bowl.

'Yes. This race does not have razors as they do not have hair. And you never have to shave again. They are very clever.'

Too damn clever! Ward thought, Eva would be still alive if they weren't such clever bastards.

Then he looked at Averin with a sudden thought. Was there something about Averin that didn't quite add up? He sat down with his bowl in silence while trying to make the vague thought clearer.

He thought: If The Great Patriotic War was about the same time in his reality as it was in mine, Averin must have been a grown man during it. I know that I age at the same rate despite these transitions. So why isn't Averin an impossibly old man?

He glanced at Averin who, catching the smile, grinned back.

Ward shrugged mentally. He didn't know anything about how these "realities" related to each other; perhaps The People were able to "harvest" their subjects from different time periods – maybe Julius Caesar was alive and well and living just down the corridor having a well-earned nap. There was one other problem with Averin that he was unable to bring into the light no matter how often he hunted down the twisting by-ways of his subconscious.

Let it go.

'So how is it going?' Averin said, breaking the silence that had gone on a little too long.

'Tough. I've seen things that I'd rather not remember.'

The other nodded. 'Da. That's the way it goes. I've seen escape from Moscow many times. Hundred times I've looked back and seen black smoke on horizon.'

'Yes, you've had a rough time. Rougher than me, I guess.' Ward felt slightly ashamed of his doubts about his companion. He changed the subject. 'So, is there anything to do for fun around here other than eat this shit?'

The other leaned forward and Ward could swear there was excitement in his eyes.

'How would you like to see outside?'

Ward's spoon stopped halfway to this mouth.

Outside? That would be exciting – day after day trapped inside a metal mausoleum was dispiriting beyond words – it felt like being buried alive. To see the wider world would be wonderful.

'Am I allowed?' he finally said, more than a little doubtfully.

'Da. They have told me because you co-operate you can have reward.'

Once again, a little jarring note. How was it that Averin was on such close terms with the Weird Ones?

Let it go.

'When?'

Averin got up. 'Now.'

With mounting excitement Ward followed his companion; it was a measure of his decline, he thought grimly, that a simple look through a window could raise such excitement.

They travelled though identical corridor after identical corridor and then Averin opened a door. Immediately strange odours amazed Ward's nostrils. He stepped through the door onto a balcony that was open to the alien air and looked around in genuine wonder.

Below him stretched the town of the Weird Ones. It was night and the multitudinous thoroughfares were picked out by yellow streetlamps, receding into the deep distance. The buildings were almost all low and rectangular but at regular intervals tall black spires reared up, impossibly high.

Even though it was night the air was still hot, as hot as Norfolk, but it was filled with strange spices and aromatic mysteries that Ward could not describe.

He walked to the low wall that marked the edge of the balcony and looked straight down.

Could a man survive a fall like that in this low gravity?

No.

But what about suicide if things got too bad?

He realised that Averin was looking at him with a slightly amused air; he had somehow been following Ward's train of thought.

'Go on – try it,' he said.

Ward leaned further over the low wall.

Was there a slight resistance then as if something was trying to hold him back?

He put his hands on the wall and heaved himself up, trying to get his upper body over the wall. It was then he felt it: a resistance as if he was trying to push himself into an invisible rubber sheet.

'Go on' Averin urged.

Ward pushed his body forward – the invisible rubber sheet became an invisible concrete wall. He could not jump off this balcony.

'Don't ask me how it works, 'Averin said imperturbably, 'but resistance is directly proportional to force applied.'

'And what does that mean?'

'More you push more it pushes back.'

84

Ward returned to his original position. There was no escape here. He looked further into the distance beyond the town where the darkness began. There on the horizon, beyond the encircling desert, he could make out the vast bulk of mighty mountains reaching up into an ebon sky.

The sky! – was it as strange as this world itself was strange?

He scanned the dark dome but there were to be seen the same familiar constellations he knew so well. He knew that from the constellations he should have been able to determine his latitude on this planet, but his knowledge of astronomy was purely descriptive.

Averin touched his arm. 'Look up my friend.' and pointed directly upwards.

Ward obeyed and there near the zenith there blazed a brilliant bluish star, easily outshining its neighbours.

'It's at opposition,' Averin said, in a sacerdotal voice, 'That's Theia.'

Ward marvelled. Theia! The rogue planet that should have crashed and formed the moon but in this reality had not. What was it like? Was it suitable for life now that it was in an orbit that presumably was intermediate between the paths that Earth and Mars had in Ward's reality? Were there deep azure seas and glaciers grinding their way down valleys to meet those seas?

And because there had been no collision with this world, this "Earth" was stillborn; too little water, too near the sun. Was this the doom that The People were trying to escape?

Ward knew that the sun was growing brighter and that therefore the habitable zone for life would be pushed out into the erstwhile dark and cold regions of the system? Could his captors be judged harshly for their attempts to avoid the cataclysm that approached?

And then Ward knew - they could be blamed, and he was blaming them. They had killed Eva as if she had been a rat discovered in the larder.

He remembered his vow: it had been made when he had thought that his enemies were the men of Norfolk; those poor, pathetic, helpless savages. Now his enemies were infinitely more potent – beings possessed of powers that those primitives could not even have imagined; creatures able to cross realities as easily as men could cross a street.

But his vow still held; it would hold whatever foes he faced.

He could not be assured of triumph: the odds were too great. But he would honour the vow he had made to the woman he had loved for such an achingly brief moment.

To Averin's amazement he raised his fist to Theia, the world that had betrayed him by allowing the Weird Ones to come into being and shouted 'Eva! I swear to you – they will pay! They will pay!'

***

The next day the investigation of Ward's brain continued. But when they reached the point where the odd little woman appeared, something different occurred – the scene was somehow replayed several times, as if there was something significant about this particular event. Ward was then forced to relive his first encounter with a Weird One and once again he stood, shocked into immobility, as a tall, spindly figure bore down on him. Then the small woman again – and again the replays. They were obviously very interested in this ordinary-looking female.

Then it ended and once again Ward sat groggily on the edge of the couch.

'So how long are you going to do this to me?' he growled, looking up at his impassive jailers, 'Will I be old and grey when you finally finish?'

The blank stares bore down on him as if they were needles piercing his skull. 'No that will not occur. When we have obtained that which we need from you, you will be killed by lethal injection. It is quite painless.'

Ward was somewhat surprised to find this new information did not really disturb him. He had always suspected that there would be no retirement home staffed by Weird One nurses attending to his every need and fetching him a nice cup of cocoa at the end of the eventless day. Death at their hands had always been the most likely outcome and he had accepted it some time ago. The only question was whether he would be able to take some with him; on the occasions when he had come up against their bodies, he was convinced that they were physically weak; the inevitable outcome of having evolved under weaker gravity than the true Earth. Just let him get his hands on some hard object that he could wield against them and he would wreak terrible vengeance on these creatures; maybe he'd be able to examine *their* brains when they were splattered on the floor.

Calm as only a man can be who has accepted the inevitable, he continued, 'I know what's got you shit-scared. Your planet is too near the

86

sun; it's going to fry and you're all going to be turned into nice crispy rashers.'

The nearest of the beings finished some adjustment to the device which had been probing Ward and turned, as usual, to stare down at him.

'We do not understand all of your words, but your basic statement is true: this planet will be rendered uninhabitable by the brightening sun. But that is no great concern; we can transfer to Theia and after that to Mars. That is not the problem that you are going to help us with.'

Ward was determined to get some proper answers out of these creatures. 'And what is your problem then, if it's not being stuck in a frying pan?'

'The Higgs boson,' came the answer, delivered in that emotionless, whispery voice that he hated so very, very much. 'There is a proof that in this probability that the Higgs is metastable and is decaying from its current mass of about one hundred and twenty-five Gigaelectron-volts.'

'Tell me something I don't know,' Ward groaned; he was back to gobbledy-gook again.

'Then you know that when that happens it will render many of the bonds in baryonic matter inoperative for life. At each point that the Higgs decays there will appear a sphere of non-existence, a sphere of annihilation that will expand at lightspeed. Eventually the entire universe of this probability will be destroyed.'

'Oh *that*!' grinned Ward, 'I thought everybody knew that!'

Chapter Twelve

'Have you ever thought about escaping out of here?' Averin enquired the next day.

Ward stopped the motion of the spoonful of yeast towards his mouth and looked sharply at the other.

'Great idea!' he sneered, 'Where in fuck's name would we go? This is another planet; in case you haven't noticed.'

Averin was unabashed. 'Into the mountains. They only live in these towns so we could be free up there.'

'And what would we eat? I repeat: this is another planet.'

'The biochemistry is almost identical to home planet. That yeast you're eating, it's native to this planet.'

How does he know all this? Ward thought, not for the first time; but he merely said: 'And what's up there to eat Mr. Encyclopaedia?'

'Small animals. They're not exactly mammals but they'd be no more difficult to catch than rabbits.'

Ward laughed out loud at that. His Norfolk skills wouldn't be entirely wasted after all.

'And we just walk out?'

'I know these corridors like Moscow Metro. I know which door leads to outside.'

Ward put his spoon down. He was resigned to death; he just wanted to kill some of The People before he went. He wanted to know if they'd show emotion as he smashed their hideous faces into pulp. Was their blood red? He wanted to know.

'I'm not sure' he said finally, conscious of how weak that sounded.

Averin leaned forward and jabbed a finger towards Ward.

'What are you afraid of? You know what waiting for you? They tie you down and stick needle in arm. And then - nothing!'

'I know that,' Ward snapped, 'And I'm not afraid.'

Averin leaned back and nodded. 'I'm sorry. I know you're not afraid of them.'

'Do you know about this Higgs thing?' Ward said, changing the subject from one he didn't want to think about at that moment.

Averin nodded. 'I understand some of the mathematics. It's about lowest energy state of vacuum dropping below zero.'

'And they knew about that in 1942, did they?'

'I have learned much from them since I have been here.'

'OK. And it would mean the end of the universe? Or just a bad hair day?'

Averin looked puzzled; he clearly did not share Ward's aversion to gobbledy-gook.

'Yes, it's a process akin to tunnelling.' (Ward nodded wisely). 'A sphere of energy not suitable for life would appear.'

'And expand at light speed.'

'Ah, I see you have been teasing me. You understand.'

'Elementary, my dear Miloslav. But what beats the crap out of me is why they think I can help them. You at least are a mathematician. I can't count beyond ten.'

'Really?' said Averin, looking slightly alarmed.

'Oh, for God's sake- haven't you heard of British humour? Have they asked for your help?'

'No. Their mathematics is much beyond what I know. They may as well ask chimp for help.'

Ward returned to his yeast, which was now only slightly warm.

'Then what in the name of all the fucks do they need me for?'

Averin nodded. 'Or me.'

***

The following day Ward was once again brought into the testing room. Without any coercion he went to the couch and lay down. The time was not yet. Every time he had come in to this place he had looked around for something loose that he could pick up and use as a cudgel on those hairless heads. But he had seen nothing. It was beginning to look as if he would have to rely on his bare hands when the time came. Did they have

89

automatic weapons? He hadn't seen any.

The images in his head had reached Norfolk. And the moment he had both hoped for and dreaded arrived: he saw Eva.

She was in his vision almost as if he was still there and she was still alive. Automatically he tried to lift his arms to embrace her – but they were pinioned to his side. He was not sure if he wept; it felt as though he had.

Once again, he saw the strange lights in the sky and bitter rage boiled through his veins. Now he knew what they were! The Weird Ones were near and were searching for him!

He knew what was coming and weakly tried to turn his head, as if that would take the scene from his vision, but his head was immobile. And it would not have helped. The vision was in his brain, not transmitted by his eyes.

He saw he and Eva recoil from the strange machine and try to get past it. He saw the Weird Ones appear on the lip of the ridge.

And he saw the blood spout from Eva's torn chest as they shot her down.

At that moment his entire body rose up, trying to break the bonds and run amok in the testing room.

But the bonds could not be broken, and he crashed back down on the couch, defeated.

That apparently ended the day's session and he was abruptly released.

For a moment the mad rage that thundered through him would have sent him hurtling at them, reaching for their throats, but he steadied himself just in time. Not yet! Not yet!

Instead he stared at them and said: 'I will kill you. I will kill you.'

No emotion was shown. It had never been shown. Would it ever?

'I do not think that will happen. Let us show you something.'

They must have realised that Ward was more than usually dangerous for one of the Weird Ones slipped behind him as another led him out of the testing room.

There was another walk down another corridor. One of the creatures was some distance in front and the other close behind. They came into another room which was filled with transparent cylinders, filled with a reddish liquid, through which streams of small bubbles were steadily rising.

90

'Go up to them,' the one in front commanded.

Ward did so and then almost recoiled.

Each cylinder contained a brain and its associated spinal cord.

'What in Christ's name is this!' he yelled, turning to the two creatures.

'They are de-fleshed brains,' was the impassive reply.

Ward turned back and looked again. Some of the brains were of a type he did not recognise but others were clearly human.

'They're not conscious, are they?' he said in a weak voice, hoping to hear a comforting answer. To be a disembodied brain in a tank and to know it! Ward knew then that there are things far worse than simple death.

'That is no concern of yours. Some of them have been removed for further study after we have administered the lethal injection. The machine we have used on you only shows us which areas of the brain we must study in more detail. We have now finished that stage of our examination of you.'

Ward knew then that when he launched his assault on the Weird Ones, he must engineer it so that there was no question of his own survival.

He must not survive.

***

Time passed with incredible rapidity as Ward realised the crisis was approaching. They had finished looking at images in his brain; the next step was the lethal injection and the removal of his brain and spinal cord. Perhaps a still conscious brain.

The stakes were now very much higher; now he had to not only kill at least one Weird One he must ensure that he perished in the onslaught. Even if he managed to find some type of cudgel how could a man cudgel himself to death? Flinging himself off the balcony wouldn't work either; there was no way he could penetrate that invisible barrier.

A deep depression came over him and he found it impossible to respond to Averin's attempts at conversation. Until another stray thought found its way into his mind.

'How come you're still here, Averin?' he demanded one day, 'Why aren't you bobbing about in a tank after an extremely heavy haircut?'

Averin shrugged. 'Not know. They still examining my brain from outside. I must have unusual type.' Ward turned away, scowling. Was that a good enough answer? The problem was that he, Ward, didn't have anything else to compare Averin against. He appeared to be the only other human in the complex.

There remained the possibility of escape.

'If we get out of this place what then?' he demanded during their next desultory conversation, 'We stand outside and are immediately mobbed by all those creatures in the town.'

'Not if we escape during day,' Averin replied smoothly, 'The People are basically nocturnal because of the great heat. We would have time to get away.'

'And cross a desert and get up into the mountains and catch a small mammal that isn't quite a mammal. Right?'

'Right.'

Ward relapsed back into a sour silence. Something was amiss here. The plan was obvious nonsense - but what was the alternative?

'The door is not locked?' he finally said, after a long, brooding silence.

'No. Only I know where it is.'

'Why haven't you escaped?'

'It needs to be two of us to help each other out. And you fellow human being – I could not leave you with these monsters."

'I'll think about it.'

And that was that. After a long period of silence Averin got up and went somewhere – presumably back to his own room.

Ward now knew how to get to the balcony, and he didn't want Averin with him; he needed to think. He knew where his companion's room was as well, but fortunately that was in the opposite direction.

He came out onto it and once again it was night. He looked down into the yellow-lit streets and he could see the small shapes of the Weird Ones moving around, far below. There were long wheeled vehicles every now and again, but the town appeared to be small enough so that few were needed.

He leaned back and lifted his head, taking in a deep, shuddering breath of the hot foetid air.

God! What a mess! Had any man ever faced this kind of nightmare before?

There in the cloudless sky Theia shone like a precious stone on black velvet; it had dimmed slightly now it was past opposition but was still a lovely sight – or would have been if Ward had been in any kind of mood to appreciate celestial beauty.

He was just about to go back inside when something buzzed past his right ear. Angrily he brushed it away. Flying pests were one problem he was not going to accept!

Then he heard it.

A faint voice said: 'Ward.'

He spun around; where was the voice coming from?

The flying insect came into view and settled on the balcony wall, not far from him.

He could see it clearly now – it was the size of a large beetle and had wings, but it was clearly metal.

'Ward.'

There could be no doubt now – the voice was coming from the beetle thing!

'What – who are you?' he gasped, hardly able to believe the reality of what was happening.

'You must escape tonight. Tomorrow they will de-flesh you. Go to the lowest floor and take the left door. Understand – the left door! I will be waiting for you.'

Ward was instantly suspicious: was this some kind of sadistic game his captors were playing? Making him think there was hope when there was none?

He needed more than voices from an unknown piece of machinery.

'Who are you,' he snapped, 'Why should I trust you?'

'You have met someone like me,' came the faint voice, 'Look!'

At that, a beam of light flashed from the beetle-thing and projected an image on the nearby wall. Ward stared in amazement. It was the woman he had encountered in the car park of Quantum Software Development.

Though, not quite, - the image was faint and flickering but he could see that this woman had reddish-auburn hair. But still he gasped: 'You!'

'Do as I say Ward. There are only two hours to sunrise. You must get out now!'

The beetle-machine's wings fluttered, it rose gently into the air – and was gone. Ward's mind whirled so badly that he had to hold onto the balcony wall for support. For a moment he thought he was going to collapse but he forced sanity back into his being.

Get out now!

But he didn't know the way.

Averin! It was time to accept his plan.

He rushed back, through the eating room, through more corridors, and banged on Averin's door.

When the occupant opened the door a crack, Ward thrust it open and forced his way in.

Averin's room was exactly the same as his. No doubt all the rooms were exactly the same.

He grabbed the Russian. 'We go! Now!'

'Now? You change mind sudden!'

'Do you know the way or not!' Ward snapped.

'Yes of course.'

'Then we go!'

They left, taking nothing.

There was nothing to take.

Down they went, down seemingly endless flights of stairs. Averin had pressed a button on the wall to call a lift but then had suddenly changed his mind and had said that the stairs were safer.

'Why safer?'

'They – they will notice electrical power surge.'

Ward's eyes narrowed. Another oddity from this odd man.

But there was no time to ponder. Down they ran, their breath coming now in great ragged gulps.

Thank God for the lesser gravity! Ward thought.

And then the stairs ended, and they were in a huge empty space.

And in the distant wall opposite were two widely separated doors.

The left one! The left one! rang in Ward's mind.

He suddenly realised that Averin was heading for the right-hand door and seized his arm to stop him.

'No, the left-hand door!'

Averin spun around, his eyes wide and staring. 'Are you mad! What do you know! Don't you trust me!'

And then it hit Ward. The thought that been buried for so long, the little worm of doubt that had been hidden in his subconscious, rose to the surface.

He didn't trust Averin.

And now he finally realised why.

'Now that you put it that way – I don't.'

Averin looked around wildly.

'They are coming! What is wrong with you Dexter?'

Ward moved closer and grabbed both of Averin's arms.

'When we first met. You came into the room and seemed surprised to see me. You said you didn't know there was another human in the building.

'So why did you say it in English!'

Averin said nothing but immediately twisted around to break Ward's grip. Ward grabbed one arm and twisted it behind Averin's back; his other arm pressed on Averin's windpipe.

'I want the truth, Miloslav my faithful companion. You're working for those swine, aren't you?'

'No no!' the Russian spluttered.

Ward twisted the pinioned arm viciously. 'The truth you bastard before I rip this arm off. Why are they letting us escape!'

'They're not,' Averin gasped, between cries of pain, 'They prefer to capture subjects when they think they've won. Adrenalin and other hormones - ahhh! – put the neurons in excited potential. Makes them - stop, stop! – easy to read – when – when – '

'When what, bastard?'

'When they de-flesh brains!'

Then everything happened at once.

The right door opened, and two Weird Ones came out. Both held handguns, though of dissimilar type.

The nearest raised his to fire.

Averin yelled 'Kill him! He's too dangerous!'

Ward twisted Averin around to face the oncoming aliens as the gun fired. He felt two slugs strike Averin in near simultaneous juddering blows. He felt the Russian die in his arms.

He dropped his erstwhile human shield and, like a tiger, threw himself on the nearest Weird One.

One arm knocked the gun out of its hand the other delivered a savage blow to its midriff. The Weird One felt as light as a papier-maché figure and crumpled at Ward's feet. Ward rolled on the floor, searching for the dropped weapon. He found it. In an instant he saw that it was based on the same universal principles as a Terrestrial handgun and, from the floor, he fired at the second Weird One. It grasped its chest, dropping its own gun. Ward saw that their blood was indeed red.

The first one was trying to get to its feet. Ward slid across the floor, grabbing the Weird One's legs and bringing him crashing down.

He sat on its thin chest with blood lust blazing in his eyes.

'Now it's your turn!'

He rammed the gun's muzzle into the creature's eye socket and angrily twisted it. Dripping red mucus, he plunged it into the other socket. He discovered then that The Weird Ones could scream as well as bleed.

He got off the writhing thing and walked over to the dead one. He picked up the other gun and briefly examined it. It was not the same type, and so to see what it did he fired it at the still living creature. A small dart appeared in its body and instantly it stopped writhing.

Ah, he thought, this is what they would have used to paralyze me before de-fleshing. The other guy was just a back-up in case things got awkward.

It was then he realised that his peril was far from over. Two of the building's inhabitants were out of the picture but there were many more. No doubt they were aware that things had gone badly wrong and were rushing reinforcements down as he stood there.

He had discovered that the Weird Ones could bleed.

He had discovered that they could die.

He did not want to discover if they had the capacity for revenge.

He thrust both guns into his belt and ran towards the left-hand door, which was some distance away.

As he got nearer, he wondered if it too would open, revealing more of his captors.

Or would he push and push on it, in increasing madness, while it steadfastly refused to open?

He reached the door and pushed.

It opened.

Chapter Thirteen

The door opened and Ward staggered out into the hot, dry night. But there was no female saviour standing there waiting to rescue him. But there were dozens of the Weird Ones who had happened to be passing when he erupted into their presence.

Of course! Ward said to himself, *the bastards are nocturnal!* As one, they fixed their gaze upon him and advanced, chattering in their own high-pitched language. Clearly humans were an unexpected and unwelcome sight on these streets. Ward watched them approach, yellow-lit in the harsh glare of the streetlamps, looking like some monstrous tribe of giant stick insects.

Then they were on him, bony hands reaching down to grab his arms and throat. Ward fought back, feeling his fists sink into soft abdomens and sending several flying with his desperate ferocity. But they were too many and slowly he sagged under the weight of their bodies. Their dreadful hissing was all he could hear.

This is it, he thought, this was all part of their scientists' plan. Now I will be dragged back in to suffer what hell they have thought up for me.

It was then he heard the unmistakeable sound of an engine revving and a small vehicle appeared from nowhere and cannoned into the throng of attackers, scattering them like skittles. Then, from his position on his hands and knees, Ward saw a pair of trousered legs approach, and a small hand reached down to help him get to his feet. He staggered up and saw that the engine noise had been produced by what looked like a small, sleek motorbike.

'Get on!' a female voice commanded as the driver straddled the bike, ready for departure. He would not have been too surprised to see the woman from the projected image but her entire face was covered by the

97

visor of her safety helmet.

Ward got on the vehicle as best he could with arms that were still trembling from his exertions. He found a metal bar behind him and had just grabbed it when the bike shot forward at an impossible speed past many prone Weird Ones; some were twitching and moaning; some were not. Buildings flashed by at an impossible rate and then abruptly there were no more. They were out in the desert. Ward found it necessary to grip the bar even more firmly as the bike began to buck and jump as it came off the road onto rough ground. Acrid dust sprayed into his nostrils and eyes, stinging like fire.

'I'm going to fall off, you stupid bitch!' he yelled into the joint roars of the wind and the engine noise, but there was no response from the helmeted head in front of him.

The land began to tilt upwards at an ever-increasing angle.

We're going up into the mountains, he thought, 'Is this Averin's plan after all?'

Just then, through a gap in the encircling hills, he caught sight of the horizon and saw that the sky just above it was suffused with an orange-red glow, which was illuminating the underbellies of wispy clouds and he realised that he had never seen this world in daylight. Was it as beautiful as the Weird Ones were terrible?

The angle of ascent levelled off somewhat and Ward noticed that the air was both colder and thinner. It had been a long time since he had felt cool air on his body, and he didn't like it.

The bike sped on with both rider and passenger in silence. Ward caught another glimpse of the eastern horizon; now the sun itself was visible behind a thin veil of cloud; an orb noticeably bigger than the sun of Earth and painted a dark, ominous crimson, like a dying coal.

Then all at once the crazy flight was over. The bike skidded to a halt in a small piece of flat land and there in front of them was a metal cube of seemingly the same dimensions as the one he and Eva had seen in Norfolk. The woman ran towards it, holding a small metal object in front of her. A door opened silently and as she was about to enter, she turned and shouted 'Bring the bike! We might need it again!'

Ward obeyed, marvelling how light the vehicle was, and entered the cube. Each wall was covered in softly glowing monitors and dials, looking like the cockpit of a passenger airliner which had been designed by Salvador Dali. She took the bike and stowed it in a locker as the door closed silently behind them. Then she faced Ward and took off her helmet.

'Ah, that's better,' she said, 'that dust gets everywhere!'

Ward was not really surprised to see the woman from the projected image and only slightly more surprised to see the woman from the carpark. But wait – no! that woman had had hair as black as night while this one had coppery-auburn hair – what was that pretentious word? – "Titian".

'Don't I know you?' he said.

'We've never met before.'

'In the Quantum Software Development carpark. But you had black hair.'

She looked suddenly interested. 'Did I? I've often wondered about going black. Did I look nice?'

Ward ignored that obvious attempt at fishing for compliments and said, 'If it wasn't you, who was it?'

She waved a delicate hand. 'Oh, that was just another probable me.'

Ward made a mental note to strangle the next person who spoke to him with meaningless sentences.

The woman suddenly said 'We can't stay here gossiping. We've got to get out before the Primans work out where we are.' and she pointed at two bucket seats near one of the walls.

They sat down and she deftly flicked her fingers over some icons on a gently glowing screen. While she was doing that Ward asked 'Primans? Who are they?'

She looked up from the screen, the soft, lambent glow sending her face into a pleasant collage of shadows and light. 'Why the inhabitants of this world – Terra Primum.'

'Why that name?'

'Well, we can't call it "Earth" because that name is reserved for the world which was formed by the merger of Terra Primum and Theia. Hence "Terra Primum" – "First Earth."'

For an instant Ward was tempted to ask about camping stoves but he did not want to be thought insane in front of this pleasant, little woman who had just saved his life. His next comment was cut off by her saying: 'Here we go. Hang on.'

And then it happened.

What happened?

Ward was never able to explain it or describe it to people who had not experienced it themselves.

The air seemed to ripple for an instant as if there had been a momentary visible shockwave passing through it. And then Ward realised that he was not alone, there were a succession of men who looked exactly like him, stretching off on his left into an indeterminate distance. And on his right, there was another series of men who looked just like him, stretching into a mirror-infinity of duplicates.

And then, as one, they turned and spoke.

'You are Ward. I am Ward. You are Ward. I am...'

And then they vanished, followed by another inexplicable shimmer in the air.

'What was that?' Ward whispered, shocked into near immobility.

'Just a consequence of our dislocation. You'll get used to it.'

'Are we safe now?'

'Reasonably safe. We're travelling through a low-probability plenum.'

Ward decided to let that pass. There was no sensation of movement, either through a low-probability plenum or anything else for that matter. Then he suddenly realised that there was one obvious question he hadn't asked. 'And what is your name?'

'Aletha.'

Aletha. Again, that similarity in sound. Was that another coincidence or was there some deeper meaning?

'A nice name.'

She beamed. 'Why thank you.'

'But why "Primans"; why use a Latin name?'

'Because my native language is a development of Latin. In your probability you would call me a "Romano-Briton"'.

Ward nodded. So far so good. He had at least heard of Romano-Britons.

'But aren't you extinct?'

'Well, in my probability the Plague of Justinian never happened, so Romano-British society didn't collapse. Hence we were able to halt the Anglo-Saxon invasions and finally absorb the settlers.'

100

Ward decided to leave it at that; he hadn't heard of the Plague of Justinian and it sounded rather nasty.

'Well, I'm very glad you're not extinct.'

At that, Aletha's semi-permanent smile became something that seemed in danger of reaching both ears, but it shrank slightly when Ward explained, 'I meant your people, of course.'

She nodded. 'Of course.'

'And now,' Ward continued, turning his chair so he was staring straight at her, 'now finally, finally you can tell me what in the name of all the fucks is going on.'

Aletha's smile wavered slightly. 'Anglo-Saxon. One hears it so rarely these days.'

'And?'

Aletha stood up and stretched. Ward found it quite unusual not to have to look upward at someone. 'And how is your theoretical physics; quantum mechanics in particular?'

'There isn't much I don't know,' he replied, with a casual shrug. He was way past caring about simple lies.

'That's good news. But,' she added brightly, 'how would you care for something to eat?'

At those words an esurient anguish struck Ward's bowels. Would you like something to eat? When had he last heard those wonderful words? He realised then he was literally starving.

'Yes, I would, very much,' he finally managed to stammer,' but do you have something other than yeast?'

There was a twinkle in Aletha's eyes as she replied: 'I have everything *except* yeast!'

Chapter Fourteen

There was certainly no yeast in Ward's meal. There was something that looked and tasted like steak (although Aletha said it wasn't) smothered in something that looked and tasted like fiery English mustard (although Aletha said it wasn't).

When Ward demanded more, Aletha tut-tutted and said 'Dexter, you've been subsisting on starvation rations for months. Your body has adjusted to that low-calorie regime. If you start ramming in everything that's high fat, high calorie now, you'll risk serious illness. Even as it is you will probably get severe indigestion.'

Ward looked up sharply. 'I didn't tell you my first name.'

'You didn't tell me your last name either. I know a great deal about you Dexter. And one of the many things I know about you is that you are no Quantum Mechanic.'

Ward's weather-beaten, sun-burnt face was quite incapable of blushing, but it is possible that he might have done so, had that been possible. 'I'm not,' he said and then grinned, 'but I can design a mean website though!'

Aletha smiled gently. 'Well that may come in useful in the struggle with the Primans; though quite how escapes me at the moment.'

Ward relaxed. Aletha was no Averin; he must stop looking for signs of duplicity. He wondered for a moment if he had been quite fair to the Russian: he knew nothing of his back story; nothing of what hold the Primans might have had over him. The man's death had been dreadful, deserved or not, and perhaps it was best to leave it there.

Further conversation with Aletha was curtailed for some time for, as she had warned, he was seized with extremely bad indigestion. Only some purplish pills that she withdrew from a small cabinet helped alleviate severe pangs.

He spent quite some time lying on a couch. Aletha had given him new clothes, including long trousers after he had complained of the cold - although she later claimed it was her idea. ('Can't have handsome young men walking around in tight shorts now, can I?' she had said, with the hint of a giggle in her voice.)

As the pains finally subsided he decided that it was time, once again, to ask for some answers.

'How long will it take us to get through this…', he hesitated for a moment, 'low-probability plenum?'

'Quite a while,' came the cheerful answer, 'after all there are an infinity of them.'

Not a good start, was his silent response to that. He walked up to Aletha and, holding both of her hands in his, looked down with what he hoped was a pleading expression and said: 'Please, please, explain to me what has happened to me.'

She looked up with a cheerful little smile. Ward was beginning to wonder what she looked like when she wasn't smiling. 'Of course. This will take some time so take a seat darling.'

'Don't call me darling.'

'Of course, dear.'

Ward lay down on the couch, his hands behind his head, and looked at the ceiling. 'Off you go. And keep it simple.'

'Of course, dear. No equations I promise.'

There was a pause as if Aletha was wondering how to begin her explanation to someone who obviously wasn't going to understand it.

'Now you know that quantum objects are described by a wave function.'

'Yes' (No point in saying "No" to the first thing she says, thought Ward.)

'One of the major problems in physics is to find an adequate explanation of how the wave function collapses. Before collapse there seem to be a range of possibilities but after the collapse, only one is actualised. How is that one state arrived at?'

Ward was lost already. 'Give me an example,' he said, hoping he didn't sound too confused.

'The classic example is Schrödinger's cat.'

Ward brightened slightly. He had heard of that unfortunate feline.

'Standard theory states that the cat is in a superposition of being both dead and alive until observed.' (Ward stole a quick glance at Aletha. She was not smiling.) 'But what constitutes an observation?'

('What indeed,' Ward murmured, nodding sagely.)

'Quantum decoherence is when one state is actualised. But what drives the selection from a range of options?'

('Good question,' said Ward).

'Many solutions have been proposed. Some have said the wave function does not have objective reality but is merely a mathematical description. Others state that the wave function is a genuine part of quantum ontology. One proposed solution is what has been come to be known as the "Many Worlds Model." This states that where there is more than one possible outcome, reality takes all of them; for example if a particle can have a clockwise or anticlockwise spin and, upon measurement, is discovered to have a clockwise spin there is another reality in which the particle is discovered to have an anticlockwise spin. Both are equally real.'

'Fascinating', said Ward, but to himself he thought: God! I'm falling asleep!

'However, the Many Worlds model in its purest form states that *whenever* an event can have more than one outcome both are actualised. The universe is constantly splitting so that all binary outcomes are fulfilled.'

Ward sat up at that point. 'Hang on, so what you're saying is that if I feel like I'm going to scratch my nose there is an entire universe in which I scratch the left-hand side and an entire universe in which I scratch the right-hand side!'

'Precisely. You've got it, you clever boy.'

Ward put his feet on the floor and stared at Aletha, who was beaming again. 'That is the biggest load of shite I've ever heard. It would mean millions of billions of zillions of universes differing in the most minute of ways!'

Aletha nodded. 'Yes, an awful lot of them. An uncountable infinity of them, in fact.'

Ward frowned. *"An uncountable infinity"*? Didn't that mean that there was a *"countable Infinity" somewhere – which was obvious nonsense!*

Aletha decided having got this far she would press on – whether she was taking Ward with her or not. 'Not all the universes have the same probability of existing, of course. A universe in which an egg is turned into an omelette is much more probable than one in which an omelette turns into an egg. But in an uncountable infinity of universes any non-zero probability will be actualised – in fact an uncountable infinity of times.'

Ward glared at her. 'Have you been taking something?' he finally said.

Aletha smiled even more broadly. 'It's counterintuitive, I know darl… Dexter. But trust me. In my probability we know all about this.

'There are probabilities in which Theia collided with Earth and formed the moon; there are probabilities in which Theia did not collide and worlds like Terra Primum came into being; there are probabilities in which Theia was so massive that the collision destroyed both bodies; there are probabilities in which Jupiter fell into the sun and all the rocky worlds were destroyed; there are…'

Ward put up a hand. 'Stop right there. Let me see if I've got this. So, everything that can happen, does happen.'

'Yes.'

'So that means that there are universes in which the Nazis won World War II; the Cuban Missile Crisis led to nuclear war…'

'Yes'

'And which you failed to rescue me and I got de-fleshed by the Primans and put in a tank.'

'Yes.'

Ward sat back down again, his legs suddenly feeling weak. He looked up at an unsmiling Aletha. 'But that's absolutely horrible! It makes a mockery of human existence! Every time something good happens there's somewhere else where something bad happens! It's the worst possible nightmare that anyone can imagine – every time that Good triumphs over Evil there's another place where Evil triumphs over Good! What's the fucking point of doing anything!'

Aletha sat beside him, this time without the hint of a smile. 'I understand your reaction, Dexter. In the end it can't be answered mathematically. We can only hope that the outcomes you describe form a countably infinite set.'

105

Ward glared at her. *And that's supposed to make me – feel better? I don't even understand what she said!*

He got up, leaving Aletha on the couch. 'OK Geek Girl – let's move on. You still haven't explained where I fit into this crazy scenario!'

Aletha's expression indicated that she didn't care for being called "Geek Girl" but she soldiered on. 'You are a very low-probability individual Dexter. Even though there are at least a countable infinity of you.'

'Stop it.'

She ignored him. 'Have you ever heard of "Quantum Roulette"? No? Well here we go - obviously in Classical roulette you will always end up dead. But if the Multiverse is real there is always a world in which you don't die as each play is a binary event. Of course, the survivor does not realise she is in a different World because she heard that her gun did NOT fire.

'But you are different. You hear the gun fire, but your consciousness ends up in a different World – *but with the memory of the previous one.* That's how you differ – darling.'

Ward stood stock still. That did seem to describe what was happening even if the explanation was the usual gobbledy-gook.

'So, I'm immortal?' he said excitedly 'Each time there's a binary choice between me living or dying my consciousness will fly to a version of me that didn't die!'

She regarded him with what was for Aletha an unusually cold expression. 'I'm afraid not Dexter. Your mind always ends in a body that corresponds to the one you were in when the binary event occurred. So, if the chance of you living or dying occurs at the time that you happen to be 101, you will end up in a body that is 101. And there's more.'

'Oh really? I didn't think I had any more party balloons that you could pop.'

'Your transitions are cumulative and chaotic, in the mathematical sense of that word. Which means that with each transition you are farther away from your original probability. Had you not noticed that there is no Terra Primum in your first world?'

'I hadn't thought of that,' Ward mumbled, 'I was too busy trying to stay alive.'

Aletha got up and slid her arm between one of Ward's and his torso. 'Of course not, you lovely man. Forgive me.'

Ward extricated his arm and moved away. 'OK. I've got most of it now. But why are the Primans chasing me? Why did they want to study my brain?'

Aletha's display of affection having not been reciprocated, she returned to the couch. 'It's complicated.'

'Oh, is that right!' Ward snapped, 'How unusual! Try me.'

'Alright. Try this. When you went to Terra Primum you did not transition into another Ward-analogue. Right?'

'Right.'

'Which means you crossed probabilities in the physical form you were in at that time. Right?'

'Right.'

'Such a feat is possible but it's tremendously expensive in terms of energy. And it can only last for a short time. It's like being a diver, you can't stay down forever; the difference here is that your original universe drags you back as if you were on the end of a very big rubber band.'

'Something to do with the Laws of Thermodynamics,' Ward ventured cautiously.

'That's a starter. Now remember about every non-zero probability being actualised?'

'How could I forget?'

'You know about the Higgs Boson?'

'Yes, the Primans told me that it's something that glues the universe together.'

'Right on the button. Well, in most probabilities it's held in a local minimum which permits life. But there is a non-zero probability that it will collapse to a lower level, an absolute minimum – taking its universe with it.'

'Let me guess – there is a countable infinity in which this happens, and all life is destroyed.'

'Something like that. The version of Terra Primum which we recently left is in such a universe. Measurements there indicate that the Higgs is collapsing.'

'So, they want to get out. I can't blame the sick bastards for that.'

107

Aletha nodded in friendly condescension. 'But don't you remember that I said that permanent physical transfer is impossible? That however much energy you expend you will always eventually be dragged back to your original location? As long as you were in their Citadel you were held in a kind of stasis by their shielding fields – but it's ruinously expensive in energy terms. So, specimens don't end to stay long there before being – being used up. Our little bug spies have seen it happen many times. Remember?'

'Indeed, I do remember that particular lecture. So what. They're stuck here. Pardon me while I wipe my tears off the floor.'

Two little lines appeared in Aletha's hitherto unblemished forehead. 'Now come on, Dexter. This really isn't too difficult. Think. I've told you that permanent physical transfer is impossible. You weren't out of the Citadel long enough to be pulled back to your most recent reality. But you would have been – and as you were outside the controlling fields you would have arrived as a disconnected cloud of subatomic particles, not as your loveable self. So why are the Primans so interested in you?'

'Do I get a holiday in Benidorm if I get this one right?' Aletha looked blank at that witticism so he continued: 'Let's see - I can't stay here permanently so I can't help them stay somewhere else permanently.' (Aletha nodded eagerly, with yet another smile lighting up her small face.) 'So, are you saying that they want to study me so they could work out how to do that transition thing like I've done - into another reality – one where the Higgs is stable?'

'That's exactly what I'm saying. Well done, you clever thing! See – you can do it!'

'But that means they'd have to transfer into a Priman analogue in our – my – world. And there aren't any – thank God.'

'But remember how I said that each transition took you further from your home reality? Eventually you'd end up in one in which your physical form was nothing like the original. As long as the host's nervous system is complex enough, transition into it is possible. That mind you have is very improbable - it has a mentalic field which stretches some distance into the surrounding space. You are definitely worthy of study.'

Whether that comment was a compliment or not, Ward ignored it. He stopped pacing back and forth and stood as still as marble. 'So, one day people in my world would wake up and find that they – were Primans?'

'Best to say that the Primans would find themselves in new bodies but in a universe with a stable Higgs.'

Ward returned to the couch and collapsed next to Aletha.

'That's one horror too many. How do we stop them?'

She put a hand delicately on his shoulder. 'That will be difficult – but between us we can do it.'

Chapter Fifteen

Ward spent some time not speaking and waved Aletha into silence when she tried to start a conversation. She looked hurt and went away to study the multitudinous control screens.

Gradually Ward came around and decided to approach her again.

'Aletha, I'm sorry. But what you've told me is hard to take. A universe in which Good can never triumph over Evil. Endless duplication of suffering – it's hard.'

She turned from the screens and looked up at him. Once again, a smile lit up her face. For the first time Ward did not find her permanent state of cheerfulness irritating.

'That's alright dear. I've lived with it all my life, I suppose. And there is another way of looking at it – it means Evil can never finally triumph over Good, don't forget.'

He sat down beside her. 'And my mind is special – but not special. I just don't get it.'

She patted his arm as if they'd known each other for years.

'Your mind is a low probability, I've said that. But the concept of probability is a difficult one when trying to apply it to infinite sets. And of course, there's your bipolarity to consider.'

Ward looked up at that word. That again.

'What about it?'

'Somehow it makes transitioning more prob – more likely. It seems to be connected with the mind having to grapple with two binary states and reconciling them.'

Ward thought about that for a while. His life had been such a whirlwind of major events of late that he hadn't been at all aware of any particular mental state.

Then Aletha's touch became firmer, more intimate. 'And that's another thing we have in common.'

'What?'

She smiled, this time a gentle smile. Her reservoir of different types of smile seemed inexhaustible. 'I'm bi-polar too.'

'You seem to be always on a high to me.'

The smile became slightly bitter. 'I deal with it as best I can. Long practice. But here's a nicer thought – my lows might coincide with your highs, so we'd be on a level all the time!'

Ward suddenly had the desire to hold this woman in his arms, to comfort her, to kiss her.

Then a thought tore into his mind – Eva!

Aletha seemed to be aware of the tension between them because for a while both parties sat stock still, gazing into each other's eyes.

To break the spell, Ward said 'Are we still travelling through the – uhh – plenum of – uhh – you know what?'

Aletha leaned back and shook her head. 'Not anymore.'

'And how exactly does one get to the end of an infinite list?' Ward was getting very tired of all this talk of infinities.

'One doesn't. But one can lift oneself out of it. Otherwise we'd never get anywhere.'

'I'm glad you mentioned that. Where exactly are we going?'

'We've been following a random path through low probabilities. We must make it difficult to be followed.'

'Followed – by whom?'

Aletha tapped his knee with careless familiarity. 'The Primans, of course. Do you think they give up that easily?' She seemed a little inclined to pay him back for that earlier moment in which nothing had happened. 'There's still a tank waiting for your brain.'

'Thanks for reminding me.'

An awkward silence fell. To break it he said. 'Are we actually moving through space?'

Aletha seemed grateful for the change of topic. 'Yes, but only as a consequence of the change in probabilities. Spatial co-ordinates are a logical consequence of the probabilities.'

'So, we could end up in the Andromeda galaxy?'

'Yes, but causality would not be violated as any message we send back would be to a different world.'

Ward threw up his hands in despair; he was beginning to feel like a performing monkey banging cymbals together.

'Look,' Aletha said, with a smile which this time held a touch of pity, 'I'll stop, and you can look out.'

She slid her chair along the space below the banked instruments and her delicate fingers flew over the screens.

'There we are,' she announced.

'I didn't feel anything.'

'Dar – uhh, Dexter, we settled into a probability. It's not like driving a car into a brick wall. Come.'

She stood up and crossed to where he was sitting. She reached down to hold a hand and pulled him upright. He did not resist her touch.

The door opened as they approached, and they stopped just outside.

Ward looked around and saw a wilderness of rock. Nothing but rock; boulder piled on boulder; small boulders; medium sized boulders, vast boulders. Stones grey; stones black; stones tawny; stones rusty. Beyond the nearby individual boulders, the drab stones merged into an inchoate mass of lithic monotony. Ward looked to the horizon. All seemed stone and just on the rim of the world he saw the grey peaks of mountains reaching up into a sky that was one featureless sheet of grey-black cloud.

'What is this Hellhole?' he said, turning to Aletha.

'Why it's Earth, Dexter. This is a probability where life never evolved. Four and a half billion years have passed and still no life has appeared.'

'It's horrible.'

'There are worse. There are Earths which are still molten after gigantic collisions with intruding planets. There are Earths where the K-Pg planetoid did not strike, and the dinosaurs prospered. And no, they didn't evolve intelligence.' Then a thought struck her. 'At least we haven't found the probability in which they have.'

'All non-zero probabilities must be actualised,' Ward announced gravely.

'You're getting it!' she said delightedly and, laughing, she turned to Ward. She was so close that their bodies touched.

He looked down at her. Her face was alive with laughter and life. He

had only to put his arms around her…

She looked up. 'Yes, Dexter, yes?' she whispered.

Eva!

He turned. 'Let's get out of here.'

He went in. She stood there for a little while and then followed.

**

They sat back in the cube vehicle, enveloped in an awkward silence. After some minutes of trying to think of something to say, Ward looked up and said 'This mentalic field business. Both you and the Primans mentioned it. What does it mean?'

Aletha did not look up from examining her hands and said dully, 'It's part of what enables you to remember the past states before your transitions. We think that any biological entity within a certain radius of your brain might be quantum entangled with your mental state and share the transition.'

Ward grunted. 'So, if I want to take my pet budgerigar along for the ride, I'd glue it to my head.'

'If you want to use such a stupid example, then yes.'

Silence fell.

Ward tried again. 'So how is it that your culture is so much more advanced than mine?'

'I told you that the Plague of Justinian didn't happen with us. So, the Eastern Roman Empire was able to conquer the western barbarians and reunite the Empire.'

'So, you've still got an Emperor?'

Aletha looked slightly puzzled. 'What other kind of government is there? We're not barbarians. Anyway, the learning of Classical Greece was not lost and was built on. In our prob…'

'Look!' Ward snapped, 'Is it remotely possible that you could utter a sentence without the word "probability" in it?'

She stood up. 'Look Ward, I know you don't like me, but do you have to be so damn rude all the time! Maybe I should have left you to spend the rest of your life floating about in a fucking tank!'

With that she spun on her heel and disappeared through a door that he hadn't noticed before in a corner of the room. Ward was left alone to wonder why he was being so unpleasant with a woman who had saved

him from a fate that was literally worse than death.

He found no answer.

When Aletha finally reappeared, he wondered if he should tough it out but finally decided to offer an apology, but it came out so clumsily that she dismissed it with a curt 'Forget it!'

She sat down in the seat in front of the main bank of instruments, and turning to him, said in clipped tones, 'Well since you've asked about my home reality, you'll soon be seeing it. The energy banks are running low and we've done enough joyriding, especially as you're not really interested. We'll be pulled back into my reality when the reserves hit zero and we have to be inside this cube when it happens, or we get out of phase.'

'Sounds unpleasant!' Ward exclaimed, trying and failing to lift the mood. Observing her stony face, he continued, 'How can you find your way around these – uhh – probabilities in any case? Could you find your way back to this one, for instance?'

'Do you really want to know, Mr. Ward?'

He winced slightly at that. 'Yes, of course.'

She looked very slightly mollified and replied, 'There are an uncountable infinity of real numbers but each one is unique. So, each probable world has a set of parameters which identify it. Therefore, in theory I could get back to this one, though if I never see it again it'll be too soon!' The latter part of her speech was delivered in a rising tone and Ward had had enough. He stood up and crossed over to where she sat, staring down at her.

'Look Aletha, you're a very nice girl and, of course, I'm eternally grateful for what you did for me back there. But you've got to remember I'm still grieving. I can't suddenly pretend that Eva was one of your bloody low probabilities, can I?'

Aletha looked down at her lap and when she looked back up at Ward her expression had softened a great deal. 'No, of course not,' she said softly, 'You wouldn't be the man you are if you could forget a woman just like that. I've seen Aoife. I've seen Eva. It's my fault. Where I come from if a girl likes a man, she just goes for him. It's the way we are. I'm stupid – I'd forgotten you're not from The Empire. Let's leave it at that.'

Ward managed a smile and thought that it would be a nice gesture to give her a peck on the cheek and so he leaned down. She didn't turn her

head, so he had to twist his own rather awkwardly to avoid her lips, but he just managed it.

'Right!' she said brightly, 'time to go before we get sucked back in a very undignified fashion. Take your seat Dexter!'

He did so and once again he found himself part of an endless sequence of Wards, as if he was trapped in an endless maze of mirrors. Before they disappeared, Ward managed to notice that as the Wards dwindled away into fathomless distance that each one was very slightly different, and the differences increased as they receded into nothingness.

But then something different happened – the air rippled again, and the Wards returned.

'I am Ward. You are Ward. I am Ward…' they chanted over and over again until Ward thought the sound of the mindless repetition would drive him insane.

The cube began to shake, very gently at first but increasing rapidly in strength until the instrument bank in front of Ward dissolved into a multicoloured blur and he heard Aletha shouting something he didn't understand.

There was an abrupt jolt and all motion ceased. The Ward multiples vanished as well.

'What the hell was that!' yelled Ward, turning his chair to face Aletha. He was shocked to see the concern on her face and felt a small stab of fear.

'I don't know,' she said quietly, 'it's never happened before.' She stabbed at the controls and a section moved up revealing a very large monitor screen. On it was nothing but blackness. A deep bottomless blackness that was somehow profoundly disturbing.

'Aren't you going to switch the damn thing on?' Ward finally muttered.

Aletha turned to him and he was shocked for the first time to see the emotion of fear painted over her delicate feature.

'It is on. There's nothing out there.'

'What do you mean – nothing?'

'I mean,' she said, rising very slowly from the chair, 'Nothing. Absolutely nothing. Not a photon. Not a neutrino. Not a virtual particle pair from the vacuum energy.'

She came up to him, looking him full in the face.

'We are where we shouldn't be. We are outside every probability that there is. There is nothing out there.'

Chapter Sixteen

'Nothing!' gasped Ward, 'I thought you said that these probabilities you keep going on about are all there is. There can't be anything outside everything!'

Aletha's lips were compressed into a thin line. 'The probabilities are confined within the framework of a meta-universe. They all share things in common which are the bedrock of reality; such as three spatial dimensions, a finite speed of causality, a system of fundamental particles such as the Higgs boson. The probabilities are all variations on that one basic theme; there are no probabilities with more than three dimensions for instance.

'And so, I repeat: there is nothing out there. We are nowhere.'

'But there can't be absolutely nothing,' Ward protested, 'We are here!'

Aletha sat down, deep in thought.

'You're right; it means that this cube is at present the entire meta-universe. It alone has a metrical framework. We have brought the fundamental particles and a space-time system with us. But such a system cannot be stable. Either the system of reality we have brought here will expand or ...'

'Or what?'

'This pocket universe will collapse. Evaporate.'

'Let's hope it's the first then.'

She looked up at him, with an expression that combined love and pity.

'Dexter darling, you still don't understand. If we expand it will be as our very own Big Bang. Our atoms will go to make up this new universe, but you and I won't be in it. You can't transition in a universe in which you are the only Ward.'

Ward sat down heavily. 'Then that's it. I'm either to be nothing or a few atoms floating about in a new universe, three billion years from now.' He looked up briefly, trying to smile. 'What a way to go.'

Aletha wasn't listening. 'How could this have happened?' she said, several times over, as if hoping an answer would materialise from the ether. She crossed the room and sat at a console which Ward had never seen her use before. Her hands flew with lightning rapidity over the screen icons and she leaned forward, chin in hand. Ward had never felt so helpless in his entire life, even when he was a captive in the Citadel of the Primans. Then there had been a possible course of action open to him, even though for most of the time he had been unable to take it. But here he had not the flimsiest shred of an idea of what to do; most of what Aletha had said to him during their time together had been meaningless, despite him nodding wisely at certain intervals. He was as helpless as the humblest laboratory animal. He looked up: she was speaking – but not to him.

To Ward's amazement a rich baritone voice was answering her. He was first astounded and then strangely annoyed that there was another male on board. And then he realised: she was in a dialogue with a sophisticated computer; one that could converse in real time.

'I calculate that an energy blast of at least seventy-five Gigawatts directed at this vessel at the instant it was lifting out of a probability would have been sufficient to knock the vessel out of the meta-universe framework,' the manly voice was saying.

Aletha nodded. 'I thought it must be something like that, but I couldn't quantify it.'

'There is an uncertainty interval around that estimate, of course,' the voice continued.

Aletha waved a hand. 'The exact value is not that significant; the mechanism is. Thank you.'

She leaned forward and the voice was no more. She sat silently for some time and when she saw Ward moving toward her, she waved at him to stop and then carried on staring into space. She pulled out another set of screens and did something very fast, very precisely.

Finally, she turned and looking him full in the eye, she said quietly: 'There is a possible way back.'

'There is?'

'Yes, but we must move fast. When we erupted into this void, we left

118

behind what I can only describe as a wake, a kind of tunnel that links *where-we-were* to *where-we-are*. But it's a tunnel of our reality that cannot exist without a metrical frame; it will be decaying at a rate I can't estimate. When that rope of reality snaps we're left with one of the two scenarios I mentioned.'

'Then we'd better stop talking and find the damn thing!'

She smiled a wan smile. 'I'm already on it my love. I've set the instruments scanning; with each second that passes they become more and more unlikely to continue working here. So, we'd better hope they find it.'

Ward sat back down. 'Well that's it. We wait to see if we become stardust.'

'The machines will alert me if they find it. But there's something you must do if we strike lucky.'

Ward's eyebrows raised involuntarily. 'There is?' Could it be that he wasn't just an inert piece of baggage?

'We must send a bolt of seventy-five Gigawatts down the tunnel ahead of us as we enter. I'll be controlling our entry as the pathway can't be more than a hundred metres wide and is steadily narrowing. You must fire the bolt when I say. Not after. Not before. When I say.'

'I don't know how.'

'Of course not. I haven't shown you yet. Come on.'

As Ward got up, he was suddenly stabbed by an intense sharp pain as if someone had just plunged a bayonet into his vitals. He cried out as he doubled up.

'What is it?' Aletha cried and then she too was hit by a stabbing pain. She grasped the side of the controls to stop herself falling. 'It's – it's the dissolution beginning!' she gasped, 'I didn't realise it would be painful!'

They hobbled to a part of the control bank that Ward had never seen used before and through gasps of pain that ominously were increasing in frequency, Aletha took him through his tasks. 'Got that?' she panted.

'I think so.'

'Don't think!' she blazed, 'Have you, or haven't you?'

'Yes.'

'I hope so or we're finished.'

Just then a powerful klaxon blasted out, cutting through the miasma of pain that was gradually enfolding them.

119

'That's it!' she cried, 'but where!'

From his new position Ward could only just see the large monitor screen. He could see nothing. Then in the exact centre there was a dim red dot.

How can we move if there's nothing to move through? he thought aimlessly but decided, not for the first time, that it was beyond his pay grade.

'Keep steady, my beauty!' Aletha yelled, surprising Ward before he realised, she was talking to the cube ship. 'The damn thing's red-shifting like Hell!'

Just then the pain doubled, then tripled. Ward felt that his intestines were being dragged out by red-hot pincers. Aletha screamed: her pain must have shot up too. He rocked back in the chair, all thought of his task lost in the screaming nightmare of agony. He had never felt anything like it: extinction would be a blessing.

'Ward!' came a sobbing voice, 'it's coming up! Listen for my call!'

Ahead of Aletha the dim red dot had widened to a huge crimson maw which seemed to be opening to swallow them whole. Its curved sides glowed as if they were entering a vast metal tube that had been raised to red heat. And yet Aletha could see that the diameter was rapidly shrinking, so fast that the bridge between *being* and *not-being* looked like it was rocketing away from them. She could no longer read the instruments through her tears; she was flying on faith now.

Ward sat still over the instruments; his body was one flaming torch of suffering. In the back of his tortured mind he knew he had to do something, but it was hard to remember what it was. Listen for a call and then press THIS! But why was it not better to surrender, to beg for release from torment, to lick the hands of the torturer in grateful submission?

Then the call came. 'Ward! NOW!'

He did not know why he had to do it. He remembered that long ago when there had been no pain that he had received that imperious instruction. He must do it.

He would do it!

He touched the icon on the screen.

And from the hurtling cube there blasted out a soundless lance of blazing, blue-white fury, a stupendous rapier of power that flashed down the exact centre of that rapidly narrowing conduit.

There was a whirl of light in eye-rending intensities.

And then darkness again.

***

The darkness slowly evaporated leaving crazy, multi-hued afterimages behind.

The eviscerating pain had gone but every cell in Ward's body ached with the bitter memory of it. He looked up, afraid of what he might see and found that Aletha was stretched motionless over the controls.

Fearing what he might find, he crossed rapidly to her side and to his vast relief found that she was breathing. At his touch she stirred slightly and, head on one side, her eyelids fluttered open.

'Dexter, the pain,' she whispered, 'the pain.'

He ran his hands over her hair, over her shoulders. 'It's gone Aletha. Gone.'

With tremendous effort she forced herself into a sitting position. 'Did – did you do it?'

He nodded. 'Yes. Well – I think so.'

She turned to the controls and ran slim fingers briefly over them and then turned to him - joy of joys - smiling.

'You did, you clever man. Right on the button. I could kiss you!'

'Well, maybe later,' Ward said hurriedly, 'But first things first – like where are we?'

She turned to the controls once more. 'Looks like we're in a normal probability. Only standard background radiation, temperatures OK.'

Ward finally relaxed, feeling his muscles starting to lose the screaming tension that they had been clamped into. 'Then we're finally safe!'

'Not so fast Dexter. What do think happened back there?'

'I have no idea. It wasn't me driving the damn thing remember.'

She gave another winsome smile and shook her auburn locks from side to side. 'My, you sure know how to compliment a girl, don't you? Well, Mr. Clever, it wasn't my bad driving, as you so charmingly implied. I wasn't applying my make-up and looking in the rear-view mirror instead of the road!'

'Then what was it?'

'Dexter, what happened is such a vanishingly low probability that my

121

people have never encountered it before. The computer and I have determined that only a directed energy flow at precisely the instant that we were lifting ourselves out of the last reality could have done it. Well?'

Dexter knew that she was expecting him to have picked up something from her last words and thought desperately for a while. Finally, he shrugged and said, 'I don't get it.'

'A directed energy flow, Brain Boy, a *directed* flow!'

'Which means?'

'That someone was directing the flow. Who might that be?'

An icy chill seized Ward's heart. 'Not the Primans!'

'Who else. You're still carrying that brain, I believe, even though it doesn't seem to be doing very much. The question is – where are they?'

'If it was the Primans what advantage was it to send us outside the meta-universe?'

Aletha looked very slightly annoyed. 'Dexter, they didn't want to do that. It was just an unlikely series of chances that came together. I'm sure that their actual intention was simply to disable this vessel.'

Ward didn't like the way this was going. 'And can they find us here – in this one reality in an endless series?'

'Dexter, you really have to start listening to me or I shall shut up. Each probability has its own unique set of parameters that define it. Our re-entry into the plenum was constrained by our point of departure; so, the reality in which we re-entered is an element in a finite set… Dexter, are you listening!'

'No. Could you just cut to the chase?'

Aletha definitely looked annoyed. 'I can't say that I'm familiar with that colloquialism, but I think I get your meaning. Short answer: They can find us. And they will.'

'For God's sake!' snapped Ward, 'Does this mean I have to spend the entire rest of my life looking over my shoulder to see if those swine are coming after me? It's like Captain Hook and the bloody crocodile!'

'I don't believe I know that gentleman,' was Aletha's smooth reply, 'But no – don't worry. We'll be safe when we're back in The Empire. Our technology is at least as good as the Primans.'

Ward tried very hard to relax after those comforting words, but it was not easy.

'When that guy spoke, I was quite shocked' he finally said.

'Oh Julius, you mean.' She looked at him under her long lashes, 'Jealous, were you?'

Ward's expression told her it was time to move on.

'He's quite harmless; in fact, I couldn't fly this thing without him. Try calling his name. I programmed him to communicate in your English – just so you didn't feel left out.'

Ward complied and immediately the deep brown voice replied, saying, 'Hello Mr. Ward. How can I help you?'

Stuck for some complex problem to offer, Ward finally said after an embarrassing silence, 'Uhh, Julius, what is two plus two?'

There was a surprisingly long pause and then Julius finally said, 'Mr. Ward, I refuse to answer that question on the grounds that it insults my intelligence.'

Aletha grinned but Ward did not.

'Great.' Ward looked around the interior of the cube. 'Look can I get out of here? I've had quite enough of being stuck inside metal boxes with no windows.'

'I advise against it. There's hardly a joule left in the banks. We'll be pulled back to my home reality very soon. When that happens, we must be inside the cube's shields otherwise we will be out of phase.'

Ward thought to himself, in insane joviality: The next time I go on one of these trips I must bring a phrasebook.

'Sorry Aletha but I'm stir-crazy. Got to get some fresh air.'

She crossed to the control bank and touched something. The door slid aside, and Ward revelled in the clean, fresh air that swept into the cube. He had readjusted to normal temperatures and the slight breeze touched his skin with hesitant fingers like the first exploratory caresses of a young virgin. The air was redolent with wonderful scents: deep, black soil, the vigour of green, growing things and the promise of cold, tumbling cascades.

Reverentially, he stepped outside and was inside what could have been a photograph from a European travelogue. There were mighty trees thrusting into a calm blue sky which was dotted here and there with fluffy fair-weather cumulus. The ground was covered in gently swaying grass, interspersed with magnificent purple flowers the size of dinner plates.

He stepped further away from the cube. Aletha's warning voice sounded from inside.

'Don't go too far Dexter! You might not be able to get back.'

She sounds like my mother! Ward thought dismissively. He noticed that at the top of the slope there was a gap in the ramparts of trees, and through which could be seen the tremendous fang of a lone mountain rearing up. The mountain was dimmed by the blue haze of distance but was that ice and snow at its tip?

He would walk up the slope and get a better view. He strode confidently up it, several times nearly tripping over large stones hidden in the grass.

Must be careful, he thought, Mother won't like me coming back with a twisted ankle.

He reached the gap in the trees and was rewarded with a view of a great, densely wooded plain, through which a mighty river meandered like a gigantic silver snake.

But the mountain was no clearer and he still could not be certain if it was snow-capped.

He glanced back down the slope: the cube ship seemed awfully far away. Best to get back.

As he turned there was a high-pitched buzzing sound and something smashed into a large boulder at his side.

Are the local beetles on kamikaze missions around here? he thought, intoxicated by the clean air and the stupendous panorama. He bent down to see what kind of beetle it was.

And what he saw sent every muscle in his body into rigid shock. The thing that lay crumpled on the ground by the boulder was no beetle.

It was a Priman paralysing dart.

They were here. Nearby.

Recovering he threw himself full-length on the ground while through his brain the single thought *Stupid! Stupid! Stupid!* reverberated over and over.

Why hadn't he stayed in the cube-ship? By now he would be safely inside the bulwarks of The Empire, no doubt being introduced to Aletha's friends and acquaintances. Now safety seemed an impossible hope.

He knew what must follow: just one dart and he would be unable to

124

move. They would lift him from the grass and take him back to Terra Primum and the Citadel; this time with no hope of escape. There he would wake to the eternal night of a disembodied state while they probed his brain, looking to understand its strange secrets.

At least he had saved Averin from that fate.

Desperate calculations ran through his mind. One thing was certain: he could not slowly crawl back down the slope to the vessel; they must be closing in on him even as he considered his options.

He had to run; perhaps the higher gravity and unaccustomed bright light would impair their aim.

No time to think more. This was his only chance.

He leapt up and ran back down the slope, trying to zig-zag his descent. Once he hit a stone and went sprawling. Still he ran on.

He got nearer the cube – and saw that something was wrong. It had a blurred quality about it as if it were a photograph that had been taken with an unsteady hand. As he approached, he could see that it was becoming translucent; the trees behind were coming mistily into view!

The phase change she had warned him about! Had there ever been a more stupid man than Dexter Ward! Then his heart leapt as he saw Aletha appear in the doorway. She would save him!

But she too was a blurred figure, like part of a watercolour painting that had been left out in the rain. She spoke but her speech was hardly distinguishable from the soughing of the soft breeze.

'Dexter! Stay here! I will come back for you!'

Almost there! The cube was just beyond his desperate fingers.

And then it vanished. Dexter was knocked over by a sudden blast of wind as the air rushed to occupy the space that had been suddenly vacated.

He lay there with his face pressed into the soft black soil, conscious of one thing.

He was alone again.

Yet not alone; he was sharing this world with an unknown number of Primans; all out to return him to the laboratory table.

Chapter Seventeen

Ward lay there for only a few moments; he knew that at any time in the next few seconds he might feel a Priman dart in his side or feel a four-fingered Priman hand on his neck.

He had to get out of this clearing, get to somewhere open where he could see the bastards coming.

He rolled over and raised himself on one knee, looking desperately about.

If only he had brought the weapons he had taken from the Citadel with him! But it had only been supposed to be a short stroll. All he had were his fists and his wits – though he now had serious doubts about the latter.

Now that the cube-ship had gone he could see that the slope continued beyond where it had been, down to a grassy plain interspersed with very large boulders. No trees but the ground was littered with large branches which must have been swept down the incline at some earlier time.

He ran again; once again trying to zig-zag as sharply as he could. He heard no more darts, but he knew that could only be a temporary reprieve. He reached the boulders; some were tall and thin like crazily slanting menhirs; others were squat and flat topped.

Weapons! He had to have a weapon!

He looked at the broken branches lying amongst the boulders and picked up the nearest. It was straight and felt very heavy and where it had broken off from the parent tree it looked wickedly sharp. He tested its strength by trying to break it over his thigh.

It did not break.

He had thought of using it as a club but maybe it would make a better spear.

He could do no more; he was certain the Primans had not managed to get behind him so they would have to come down the slope.

And so they did.

There were three of them, all carrying small handguns. Ward could not be certain at this distance, but he had no doubt that they were the paralysing type.

All his hatred and anger came flooding back as he saw his weird foes again. He could not say why, but the one in the rear seemed subtly different.

How could he destroy them with just a stick?

Even as he thought that, he became conscious that the light was rapidly fading, and the air was getting colder.

Oh no! he thought in gathering despair, in the night they'll have the advantage over me!

But then he realised that the sun had been quite high when he had last seen it. Then something soft and light hit him on the head.

He looked up.

Storm clouds were rapidly filling the sky, clouds with black swollen bellies from which large drops were already starting to fall. In the distance there was a brief lightning flash.

Rain! He remembered that Averin had told him that on Terra Primum it only ever rained in the mountains. The Primans would be unused to rain.

Could he turn that to his advantage?

The rain began in earnest; cold, grey, slanting curtains of icy water that reduced the visibility to nearly nil.

Ward shivered under that onslaught of cold.

Yes, you bastards! he thought, you're not used to cold, are you? Come to me – come on!

He hugged the lichen-scabbed side of a boulder in a crouching position, his makeshift spear at the ready. He could not hear footsteps in the thunder of the downpour, but his eyes roved ceaselessly, trying to penetrate the grey gloom.

He saw one!

It was above him on the slope and apparently alone.

He drew back his spear. It was then he remembered that doe he had seen in the sun-smitten wastes of Norfolk, an eternity ago. He remembered how at the time it had seemed so important that his aim was true. How trivial that incident seemed now!

He drew back the spear, remembering to compensate for the downdraft of the cloudburst. He sent it flying across the rainy interval that separated them.

It caught the Priman in the throat as he had intended but it was not a killing blow.

The Priman dropped its weapon and fell to its knees, hands scrabbling at the spear, trying to remove it. Ward crossed the gap in a loping run, keeping his body as low as possible. One kick sent the Priman onto its back and then he pulled the spear out of the creature's neck, the hot blood covering his hands. He spared no time to look into his enemy's face but plunged the spear back down, this time deep into its neck. There was a choking cry and then all was still.

In his triumph Ward forgot to stay low and reared up, waving his spear. It was then he felt a tiny bite on his arm and looking down, saw a paralysing dart protruding from his left bicep. Instantly he pulled it out and threw it as far away as possible. He looked again at his arm: the material of Aletha's Empire was strong and resilient – the dart had hardly penetrated it. Surely only a microgram of the drug could have made its way into his bloodstream. What could a microgram do?

He was about to find out.

He dropped the spear and took two guns from the dead Priman's holsters. As before one was the paralyser; the other a conventional killing weapon. He backed up against the sheer wall of the nearest boulder and slid down it, keeping the gun upright.

Then he felt it. Every motion slowed down, and the smallest movement seemed to be struggling against a tremendous resistance. Even his blinking seemed to take minutes and the eyelids felt like they were glued to his face. The light, already dim, faded to near black and the hand holding the gun very slowly dropped until it was pointing into the sodden ground.

This is it! Ward thought.

But as he sat there, slumped in the downpour, he thought Were the Primans so bad?

They were faced with annihilation – was it surprising that they would try any stratagem to escape ineluctable oblivion? Would human beings have done any better?

128

Primans and humans – brothers in adversity – both struggling against an indifferent universe that not only did not care about their suffering but was not even aware of it.

Primans and humans. Both courageous in facing their fates – one being swept out of existence by an ever-expanding sphere of nothingness; the other being cooked alive in the oven that was a despoiled Earth. To serve the Primans was a noble end and a fitting conclusion to his hitherto pointless life.

It was then that he had a vision of Eva. Once again, he seemed to see the Primans come over the lip of the ridge and without any attempt at communication, any attempt at co-operation, to gun her down without a second's hesitation.

Strength seemed to sweep back into him, strong and potent, like molten iron pouring from a cupola into its mould.

He opened his eyes to find a Priman face less than a metre from his own.

He lifted the gun and fired into the face.

It fell out of his vision in red ruin as he shakily straightened himself.

Two down; one to go.

But the rain was abating: his major advantage would soon be gone.

But he had the Priman killing gun and he knew how to use it.

Shelter! He must find shelter. He had just had the narrowest of escapes from the paralysing weapon and his limbs still felt as if they had been transformed into concrete. Every step he took he sank ankle deep into clinging black mud and it seemed to take all his strength to pull his feet out.

He came to the widest of the great boulders and crouched behind it.

How long could he keep this hide-and-seek game going?

Just then he heard a voice; a powerful, booming voice. It sounded like a Priman voice but impossibly louder.

Then he realised: it was a Priman voice but electronically amplified.

'Ward! Ward! There is no need for this stupidity.'

Where was that voice coming from? Amplified as it was, it seemed omnidirectional.

'I mean you no harm.'

At that Ward could not resist answering. 'That's why you're trying to vivisect me!'

'No, that was a mistake on our part. We have non-invasive techniques now to understand the unusual powers of your brain. You will not be harmed.'

'Bullshit!' roared Ward, 'Why were you trying to capture me then?'

He listened carefully then to see if he could hear the squelching noise of Priman feet trying to creep up on him. There were none.

'That was the stupid foot soldiers they forced me to bring along. They disobeyed orders. You saved me some work by killing them. I would not have been so merciful.'

Ward thought: It's not easy trying to pretend that you're a nice guy when you're obviously not.

'What's in it for me?' he yelled, hoping that the next answer would give some indication of where this Priman leader was.

'You will have great honour among The People and be given everything you want. There are females of your race on Terra Primum. Perhaps you didn't know that.'

For an instant Ward was shaken by the revelation that there were women among the captives on that world but then the full implications of the Priman's words sank in.

'I had a woman,' he screamed, 'and you killed her!'

'The stupid lower castes again,' came the booming voice, 'it was all so unnecessary. Ward, you know nothing of our history, of our struggle to tame a hostile world and build a great civilisation. And we are to be exterminated by a blind chance! I think not!'

Where is he! Ward thought with growing madness. He spun around suddenly.

The Priman was not there.

'Look Big Shot,' he yelled again, 'it's no deal! You've learned your lines so well I could almost break into tears. But I made a vow to kill every Priman I could find and by all that's holy I'm going to do it!'

He ran then from one boulder to another, looking up the slope, with the gun raised, to where he was sure the Priman must be.

He was not there.

The great voice came again.

'Very well Ward. I have tried reason, but it would seem that such a

130

discipline is beyond you. But do you think we are primitive savages because we don't look like you? Let me tell you that we are well aware of Secundo Terra and the Roman Empire. It may be to there that we shall transfer our consciousnesses when we have finished studying you. The planet will need some engineering, but it will make a fine home.'

Ward was frozen with horror at that thought – Aletha's body becoming a mere receptacle among a world population of human vessels into which these creatures would pour their minds!

'One more thing you deluded creature. The female told you that she would return, I believe. Perhaps she did not take into account the different time flows within the probabilities.

'Or perhaps she forgot to tell you that a few minutes on Secundo Terra will be over a hundred years here! You will never see her again.'

Ward had suffered many blows in his recent past but this one so unnerved him that he let the gun slip from his fingers into the mud.

Never to see Aletha again!

'I know exactly where you are hiding Ward and I could come down and collect you now. But I want you to come to me of your own free will. If you do, then I promise you that you will get everything you could ever want among The People, and that includes access on demand to your females.

'But I warn you: Come to me soon or de-fleshing will be your reward.'

Against his will Ward heard himself saying: 'How will I find you?'

'Simply return here and lay any weapons you have at your feet and I will come to you. This planet has the same rotation period as your own. You have exactly twenty-four hours. If you are not here then, I will hunt you down and harvest you. I am not sure which course of action will give me the greatest pleasure.'

Silence swept over Ward like a great wave as he slumped to his hands and knees beside the great boulder.

No way out! This time, there was no way out!

He crouched there for some time, staring down into the mud as the light gradually faded around him. When he finally lifted his head, the first stars were beginning to shine in the deep blue sky.

His rain-soaked body began to shiver as the temperature started to drop, as night wore on. He had not the slightest idea of what to do; he was not as adjusted to cold as he had believed, and he was suddenly conscious of ravenous hunger tearing at his innards.

Why wait? Why not simply shout 'I surrender!' and trust that the Priman leader would keep his word. A life without pain on Terra Primum in return for allowing them to study him – what was so bad about that?

But he thought first about Eva and then he thought about Aletha. The first was beyond all harm the Primans could do but the second was not.

The leader had said he would hunt him down – very well: he accepted that bargain.

There was some chance there. In a physical confrontation he would have the edge; the other would be in the same position as a man facing a chimpanzee – bigger but with muscles that were no match for his opponent.

And maybe if there was one bullet left – there was one place the Primans could not reach.

He began the long trudge back up the slope, the muddy gun clutched in his right hand.

He found a hollowed-out tree trunk and covering himself with ferns and dead leaves began a fitful night's sleep.

***

Dawn finally came and with it Ward began to move cold-stiffened limbs. The heaviness caused by the paralysing drug had worn off but had left a constant electric tingling.

He had no idea what to do next: he found some berries hanging from a bush and not caring whether or not they were poisonous, wolfed them down. Some water in a hollow at the top of a rock provided him with a drink. Before he plunged his hands into the water, he saw his reflection staring back. It was a haggard, hollowed-out face with haunted eyes that stared back; the face of a man who had suffered too much, been forced to make too many life-or-death decisions. However, the oddest thing about it was the perfectly smooth chin – the result of the Priman drug.

He began looking for footprints thinking they could lead him to the Priman's lair. Perhaps he could catch the leader in whatever form of sleep they took and kill him.

He did indeed find some footprints at the top of the slope, but they disappeared when they reached firmer ground and Ward was not tracker

132

enough to find any more clues to the being's whereabouts.

In all his wanderings, he saw no sign whatsoever of any other presence, human or otherwise; this probability, so like his Earth in every other way, seemed totally uninhabited.

He decided that there was no point in wandering; he was merely wasting strength that he would need for the coming battle.

He stopped at the top of a ridge not far from where he had made his fateful error when his eyes caught the flash of metal that a fleeting sunbeam had picked out.

He walked slowly down the slope, keeping his eyes fixed on where he seen the metallic flash. After some time, he parted some bushes and what he saw made his heart leap with joy.

It was a little difficult to be sure, but it certainly looked like a cube-ship.

Aletha! Oh, my girl, how he would kiss her!

With new strength he hurried through the undergrowth in its direction.

Closer!

Nearer!

Aletha!

He burst through some especially dense undergrowth and came upon the cube.

And once again his heart sank.

It was a cube-ship certainly- but the metal had a gold-amber glow that he knew so well.

It was a Priman ship.

He retreated back into the undergrowth and was about to turn his back on the vessel and retrace his steps when a thought stopped him.

This was what he wanted! He had found the leader's lair.

He would wait until the creature emerged and kill him.

And so, he lay there, while the sun climbed higher and large black flies seemed to find him a very attractive meal.

Eventually despite all his best intentions he began to doze.

It was then a large shadow fell over him.

He suddenly found himself jerked to his feet by a large hand. Instantly awake, he saw a Priman face staring down at him. But there was something different about it. It was larger and wider. And the grip was stronger.

'Ward,' came the voice, which was also more powerful, 'I told you to

133

lay down weapons, but you have not done so.'

Even in his confused state, Ward realised that he was in the grip of a different type of Priman; that the leader's reference to castes among them was not purely a social concept – there was an upper caste of Priman which was physically more powerful!

'I will release you now for I want to see you give yourself up to me in your final despair. The longer you take the shorter will be the time before we terminate you. Go now Ward. I will come for you at midnight at the place of boulders.'

And with that the leader sent a blow straight onto Ward's chin, knocking his head back violently. Then he felt powerful arms lifting him up straight so the terrible face of the Priman stared directly into his own. Once again, Ward smelled the rotting fish stench of the creature's breath.

'I am tempted to withdraw my offer of leniency, but I am a leader of honour. I will not withdraw it. But I warn you – go!'

And with that he flung the human into the undergrowth.

Ward reached for his gun – and found himself staring into the muzzle of that of the leader.

'You are not an honourable creature, it seems. But I am merciful. Go!'

Ward went, with burning rage in his heart – but also a new fear.

Chapter Eighteen

Ward pondered his new situation. He had been prepared for a showdown with the surviving Priman but he had expected to have a significant physical advantage over it.

He had not expected the creatures to come in different versions, with one seemingly as strong as an average man. And suffering from cold and hunger as he was Ward wondered if he, himself, was still an average man.

But still he had the feeling that he was missing something; that he had overlooked a vital part of the situation.

He still had the standard handgun he had taken from the foot-soldier Priman. What was to stop him simply waiting for the leader to come down the slope to the place of boulders and just gun him down?

Could it really be that simple?

Then as he went over and over the coming scenario in his mind a terrible suspicion began to dawn. He took out the gun and stared down at it. It was a beautifully made piece of kit and even though it had been designed for non-human hands it fitted superbly well in his own. How many shells did it contain?

He knew of only one firing; the one he had made. He could spare one for his experiment to check his suspicion. He lined the weapon on a nearby tree and pressed the trigger.

Nothing. Not even a click. The thing was a completely inert piece of metal. The leader's confidence was explained: obviously he had the ability to remotely control his subordinates' weapons.

Ward now knew that defeating the leader would be a vastly more difficult enterprise; somehow, he had to get close enough to engage it in hand-to-hand combat.

Ward had fought men in Norfolk and won, so it was not impossible;

135

the being was stronger than average but it was no superhuman.

Morosely he trudged down the slope he had ascended on that fateful day and sat looking at where Aletha's cube-ship had been. The grass was still compressed where it had sat.

Not for the first time he bemoaned his stupidity and wondered what the dear woman saw in him.

They had had safety in their grasp and he had thrown it away. When she returned in a hundred years, she might find a few pieces of bone hidden among the grass – and that would be all that was left of Dexter Ward; Profession: Idiot.

As he stared at the depression in the grass it seemed that there was a blurring in the air above it and then the ghostly outlines of a structure gradually began to take form before his astounded eyes.

Green lights flashed through the zenith and down to the horizon.

The hairs on his body began to rise up as if caught in a powerful electric field.

A cube-ship was entering this probability!

Ward tensed – was this reinforcements from Terra Primum?

He flung himself flat and watched as the vessel gradually materialised.

To his unbounded joy it had the silvery sheen that identified it as a vessel of The Empire!

Hardly daring to hope, he watched the machine assume full solidity and waited to see who the occupant was.

The door opened.

It was Aletha!

She was dressed slightly differently but it was the same woman.

She stood at the entrance to the cube and shouted: 'Dexter! It's me – Aletha! Are you here like I told you to be?'

He leapt up and ran headlong towards the vessel shouting' 'I'm here!'

He was slightly surprised to see the look of elation on her face as if she was welcoming back a conquering hero instead of a complete dimwit. They embraced in the doorway and Ward kissed her for the first time. After a few seconds he made to pull away but found that Aletha was keeping his lips firmly plastered to hers. When she finally released him she smirked and said, 'Mmmm. That was good. We must do it more often!'

'Aletha!' he said, cutting through her beatific feelings, 'We've got to get

136

out of here — now!'

She looked puzzled. 'Why? - this probability is uninhabited.'

'There are Primans here,' he panted from his recent sprint, 'A special one – a leader type!'

Her expression changed instantly from joy to concern. 'I see. Better close the ship up then. Come on in.'

Ward followed and they sat down looking at each other.

She leaned forward and took his hands in hers.

'The door is secure now darling. They couldn't get through that with a cannon. It's so good to see you again!'

'Yes, it is pleasant to see you again, Mr. Ward,' came Julius's powerful voice.

'Don't get me wrong,' Ward finally said, 'but I wasn't expecting to see you again. The Priman said you wouldn't be back for a hundred years – something about "time streams".'

She giggled. 'Oh – that old thing! We solved that a long time ago. I just asked Julius to compensate and he did it – no trouble at all!'

'That is not strictly accurate,' Julius commented, 'it was not a trivial exercise.'

'I'm very glad to hear it – and very glad to see you, Aletha,' Ward replied, feeling the tension sweep out of him. He felt as though he could sleep for a month. Over and over he told himself that there would be no final confrontation with the Priman leader – he was safe at long last! He felt weak and exhausted but happy.

'We'll be underway shortly,' Aletha said, 'and back in The Empire. Mother is really looking forward to meeting you!'

'The Empire? Mother?' Ward echoed weakly, 'you mean you can't take me back to my original probability? London and all that?'

'Come on now Dexter. There's nothing for you there but a woman who wanted to murder you. Stupid cow. And London was a Roman foundation, don't forget. There's a London in The Empire. A magnificent city!'

Ward pondered for a moment. She spoke the truth. There he had lived a grey life in a grey urban jungle; haunted by his downswings and with no hope for anything better.

This woman seemed to think he was a human being worth cherishing;

God knew why!

'I'm not very good at languages. Human languages that is. All those – what do you call them – declensions.'

She patted his knee consolingly. 'Latin has moved on a lot. It's more like Spanish now.'

Ward was not entirely sure if that was particularly reassuring but then all thoughts of languages were driven away.

They heard the door open.

They both spun around and both saw the Priman leader standing in the doorway. It came in and placed a small metal object on the side of the control bank.

'Clearly I have underestimated The Empire's scientific development. You have obviously solved the time stream misalignment problem. The Ruling Council will be very interested to hear that. But fortunately, you have not updated the codes that control the doors of your vessels. Hence, my presence here.'

Aletha's face was white and drawn. She looked unrecognisable.

'What do you want here?'

'What we have always wanted. We want Ward. Or a part of him at least. We do not know how long it will be before our home probability is destroyed but it cannot be that long. The unique qualities of Ward's brain will save us. We will be able to permanently transfer our consciousnesses to a safe probability and Priman culture will be secure for all time. Once we have made our new home secure there will be time enough to investigate the great task of colonising other quantum realms. The Empire will be a formidable foe but given time we will be able to occupy it.

'But Ward's brain is the key to it all. We must have it.'

Ward noticed that the leader's other hand was holding a gun – no doubt a fully-functioning gun.

'You can't expect me just to hand Dexter over!' Aletha cried.

'I don't expect you to do anything. I expect Ward to voluntarily give himself up and come with me.'

'And why would I do that?' Ward snarled.

The leader waved his gun at the two humans. 'This is a very powerful weapon. Powerful enough to turn the metal of your controls into scrap. Think of what it could do to soft flesh. Ward, you can either come with me now or you can spend some minutes examining the contents of this female's torso. And then you still come with me. Rest assured Ward, if you are thinking of attacking me I will fire to disable you. You will not escape into death.

The choice is yours. From my point of view the outcome will be the same. But not from the female's point of view.'

Ward stared at the creature from another world. He measured the distance between them in his mind and calculated the odds of him getting to the Priman before it fired.

Zero.

'Be quick, Ward,' came the hissing voice. 'I am anxious to see the world of The People again. These cold, wet places irritate me immensely.'

Ward could not move; his muscles seemed frozen as he grappled with indecision.

All he knew was that Aletha did not deserve to die simply because she had met him.

The Priman leader raised its gun. 'Time up. Perhaps you are interested in female anatomy.'

Then Ward knew what he must attempt.

In a roaring voice he commanded: 'Julius! Kill the Priman!'

Julius began to speak, no doubt to explain his inability to accomplish that task.

It did not matter.

Automatically, the Priman had turned to locate the other male in the room.

A slight motion, but enough to make a final throw of the die worth the attempt.

Ward threw himself across the intervening space onto the Priman and the force of the collision knocked it to the floor. He grabbed the arm with the gun and tried to wrest it from the creature's grip.

No good – it held on.

They rolled over and over. The gun fired, hitting the control panel with a shower of crepitating sparks. Julius's voice was cut off in mid-expostulation.

'Get down Aletha!' Ward roared.

Now he was on top and he rained blow after blow onto the leader's face. Blow after blow after blow.

Perhaps it wasn't so strong after all.

He thought of Eva and her love for him. How they had killed her like swatting a fly.

He hit down again with maniacal strength.

He thought of the brains in the cylinders on Terra Primum.

Again, he struck.

'I'm going to kill you!' he screamed through the mayhem. There was a sound of electrical crackling behind him and the ominous stink of burning.

He thought of Aletha and the cold indifference to her life that the thing below him had shown.

He thought of the Primans' dreams of colonising the realities.

The bloodied thing managed to twist its arm from Ward's grip and the muzzle of the gun crept closer and closer to Ward's face as he battled to hold it down.

Again, it fired. Ward felt the heat as the bullet passed his cheek with millimetres to spare.

Again, there was a cascade of sparks, showering down on the combatants.

Behind Ward, Aletha screamed.

That was enough for Ward – the thought of Aletha being hurt poured strength into him from some unknown reservoir of power. He tore the gun from the leader's grasp seemingly without effort. This weapon he knew had not been deactivated.

He looked down at close range at the thing's smashed features and calmly placed the muzzle between its eyes.

'I've had enough of you bastards,' he said quietly, 'Now die.'

Then he fired.

After a few seconds, when he had wiped the mess from his face, he fired again.

And again.

Shaking from head to toe he staggered to his feet.

He was suddenly aware of flames leaping from floor to ceiling behind Aletha. The cube-ship was on fire.

Aletha ran towards him, her expression a strange mix of simultaneous fear and joy.

'Dexter, we've got to get out. The whole thing's going to go up!'

Ward nodded and turned to the door. It was shut.

Just then a peculiar vibration passed through the air like a visible shock wave.

Immediately he became the central figure in a line of Wards stretching off to infinity on the left and infinity on the right.

'You are Ward. I am Ward. You are …' they chanted moronically.

The cube-ship was lifting out of this probability!

But this was no smooth transition; the vessel lurched drunkenly from side to side like a small ship in a typhoon.

'What's happening?' Ward yelled, through a rapidly increasing cacophony.

'I don't know,' came Aletha's frightened reply, 'Julius is dead and without him I can't control the ship!'

The vessel then turned literally upside down, leaving the two live occupants clinging for their lives to the chairs. The Priman corpse hit the ceiling with a vile squelch.

The ship up righted itself and then there was a sudden cessation of all sense of movement. The Priman corpse resumed its original position.

'Have we dropped into another reality?' Ward gasped. The room was rapidly filling with tarry black smoke which was forcing its way into his lungs with burning talons.

'I don't know!' sobbed Aletha, 'None of the instruments are working!'

New reality or not, Ward knew that they had to get out or their lives would be measured in minutes; whatever was out there – they had to get out! He ran to the door and pushed hard against it.

Jammed.

He bent down and through the small gap between door and jamb he could see a piece of metal that shouldn't be there. He lifted the Priman gun – how many bullets left?

He had no idea.

He fired through the gap at the metal strip and it burst into sparkling fragments. Once again he slammed against the door and with a groan of tortured metal it opened somewhat but then stopped.

Ward looked at the gap. Aletha could get through – but could he?

He grabbed her from where she stood just behind him and pushed her into the gap. Jagged metal tore at her blouse, leaving red lines on her pale skin.

'Go on!' he roared, 'Go on, damn you!'

To his immense relief she disappeared into whatever lay beyond.

It seemed very noisy out there but to remain in the cube-ship was certain death.

Outside was merely probable death.

Probabilities! thought Ward, How I do hate probabilities!

He approached the gap. It was very narrow with wicked, jagged edges.

No matter. The flames had spread over the ceiling and blobs of semi-molten material were beginning to sprinkle down on him. The air was rapidly becoming one black, unbreathable inferno.

He forced his way into the gap. The metal cut into him, more deeply that it had into Aletha due to his greater bulk. He did not cry out – he was long past reacting to minor physical pain. The tough Imperial material shielded him somewhat, just as it had saved him from the paralysing dart. But it hurt!

And then he was out. The sudden cessation of resistance to his efforts caused him to fall heavily on the ground. As he lay there, his face yet again buried in the soil, he was aware that the ground was shaking violently.

He rolled onto his back – and was rewarded with a vision of Hell.

Stretching almost from horizon to horizon was a vast reddish globe, so close to the surface that it had been transmuted into a terrible louring dome. Great swirling, parallel bands of cloud were visible, lit from within by flickering lightning flashes. Waves of heat were apparently emanating from it, causing bushfires to rage all around them.

Ward felt strangely light as if something was pulling up towards those stormy cloud belts.

Which there was.

'What's happening?' he gasped, each breath sucking furnace air into him, 'What is it?'

'It's a brown dwarf!' Aletha yelled, through the chaotic tumult, 'it must be passing through this Solar system – and close to this Earth!'

She came close to him and put her arms around his neck.

'Dexter this is the end for me.'

Ward stared at her smut-smeared face. 'What are you talking about.

You'll be pulled back to The Empire, won't you?'

Her smile was wistful, full of a lifetime of suffering; of unrealised hopes.

'No, my darling. The heat will fry me long before then. And even if it doesn't – I can't get back to The Empire when I'm outside the ship.'

She pointed at the vessel which now had hungry flames coming out through the gap through which they had escaped. 'I'm afraid mother will never meet you now. I'll never have you to myself. It's goodbye Dexter. I'm sorry we couldn't have had more. You are safe though, my love, you will transition to safety.'

Dexter rocked back on his heels. The bushfires were closer. Small stones were levitating around them and in the distance there were gargantuan rumblings as the very planetary crust was beginning to splinter in that tremendous gravitational potential.

No! No! he cried within. Not again! Not another tragedy because of these bloody probabilities.

Finally, he knew what had to be done.

'No,' he said firmly through the howling madness of the world-girdling storm, 'I am not losing you. There is a way.'

'What way?'

They had to be very close now because of the roar of the crashing rocks.

'The mentalic field. The budgerigar. Don't you remember?'

She looked wild-eyed up into him. 'You're going to kill me?'

'Kill the two of us. You have to be very close. Come put your head against mine. Hurry.'

She placed her right temple against Ward's left temple.

'This shot will be powerful enough to go through both skulls,' he assured her, 'there will be no pain.'

'Dexter, I'm frightened!' she whispered as she sat next to him, head touching head.

He suddenly thought What if I've used the last shot?

He looked back up at the giant world that was tearing this Earth to shreds and snarled in his whirling mind: Goodbye bastard! This time you don't get me!

He fired.

There was a terrible noise, a feeling of intense heat and redness filled his vision.

***

Ward was afraid that Aletha might be dead but she was not.

He opened his eyes to find he was lying on a slope covered in fine feathery grass and dotted with flowers in all the colours of the rainbow and many more that are not in the rainbow. The sky was a deep, vibrant blue.

They were wearing close fitting clothes that seemed to change colour as they moved.

Aletha was lying beside him with her eyes closed but the fall and rise of her bosom revealed that she lived.

The Priman gore had gone from his face so he lowered his lips to hers and gently kissed her. Her eyes opened slowly and he saw yet again that smile he had feared he would never see again.

'Dexter – you did it. We're alive.'

'Only because I was told about something I hadn't heard of and didn't know I had.'

She sat up and they hugged each other.

'But where are we?' she said eventually. 'This isn't The Empire.'

They looked around and in the near distance they could see a large city with many graceful spires and sparkling domes. Above the city were shapes that looked like hot air balloons - but could not be by the way they moved: swiftly and purposely.

'I don't know,' he said, feeling his lips curl into an unaccustomed smile. 'But it looks like a good place to end up in.'

She pulled his sleeve and said: 'Dexter, I want to say something to you. Listen to me and don't be angry.'

'Ok.'

'I know you loved Eva and she loved you, but Dexter, if a man can love once he can love again, surely? Loving someone else doesn't mean that you forget the other or stop loving them. Love is such a rare thing that it can't be passed over and left to waste.

'Dexter, I, and other probabilities of me, have followed you through all these quantum states. We have all loved you because we know what kind of man you are. You have suffered greatly, more than most men could

144

bear, but you have not lost your humanity, your capacity for love.

'And listen: Aoife, Eva, Aletha – don't you see the pattern? Dexter, it's me you've been searching for through the realities. Me - just as I've been searching for you!'

She stopped and drew back a little, as if fearing that she had said too much.

Ward sat silently for a while, wondering if he was angry at what she had said about Eva.

Gradually he came to realise that he was not angry and that a man can love more than once.

And so, he turned to her and they kissed, kissed properly for the first time, but not the last.

Later they began the long trek to the great unknown city that lay below them.

And in the fullness of time Ward and Aletha were accepted into the ranks of The Great Ones of the mighty civilisation of the Nalendi.

THE END

Lightning Source UK Ltd.
Milton Keynes UK
UKHW010708160220
358798UK00008B/254

9 781916 161962